"Are you going to try to get me into bed afterward?"

"No," Jason said with what he hoped was an honest-sounding conviction. "No, I wouldn't do that."

"Why not?" she posed in a puzzled tone. "You said you found me pretty and desirable. You also asked me to marry you. I imagined you fancied me, at least a little."

"I *do* fancy you. And more than a little, Emma."

"It's perfectly all right, Jason. I've been brought up in a country town, not a convent. I just didn't want to give you false hopes if I agreed to go out to dinner with you. You're a very attractive, experienced man, and I'm sure you know how to get a girl. But I have no intention of sleeping with you, not this side of a wedding ring, anyway."

Some of our bestselling writers are Australians!

Helen Bianchin...
Emma Darcy...
Miranda Lee...

Look out for their novels about the
Wonder from Down Under—
where spirited women win the hearts of
Australia's most eligible men.

THE AUSTRALIANS

He's big, he's brash, he's brazen—he's Australian!

Miranda Lee

THE VIRGIN BRIDE

THE AUSTRALIANS

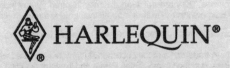
HARLEQUIN®

TORONTO • NEW YORK • LONDON
AMSTERDAM • PARIS • SYDNEY • HAMBURG
STOCKHOLM • ATHENS • TOKYO • MILAN • MADRID
PRAGUE • WARSAW • BUDAPEST • AUCKLAND

ISBN 0-373-12278-0

THE VIRGIN BRIDE

First North American Publication 2002.

Copyright © 1999 by Miranda Lee.

Visit us at www.eHarlequin.com

Printed in U.S.A.

CHAPTER ONE

WHAT a glorious day, Jason thought as he stepped outside. Spring had finally come, and with it that delicious sunshine which encompassed just the right amount of warmth. The town had never looked better, nestled at the base of now lush green hills. The sky was clear and blue. Birds twittered happily in a nearby tree.

Impossible to feel discontent on such a day, Jason decided as he walked down the front path and out onto the pavement.

And yet…

You can't have everything in life, son, he heard his mother say.

How right she was, that wise old mum of his.

His heart turned over at the thought of her, and of her wretched life: married at eighteen to a no-good drinker and gambler, the mother of seven boys by the time she was thirty, a deserted wife by thirty-one, worn out and white-haired by fifty, dead five years ago of a stroke.

She'd only been fifty-five.

He was her youngest, a bright and affectionate boy who'd grown into a discontented and fiercely ambitious teenager, determined to be rich one day. He'd gone to medical school not because of a love of medicine, but because of the love of money. His mother had worried about this, he knew. She'd argued that money wasn't the right reason to become a doctor.

How he would like the opportunity to tell her that he'd finally become a good doctor, and that he was quite happy, despite not being rich at all.

Not perfectly happy, of course. He no longer expected that.

'Morning, Dr Steel. Nice day, isn't it?'

'It surely is, Florrie.' Florrie was one of his patients. She was around seventy and popped into the surgery practically every week to discuss one of her wide range of ailments.

'Muriel's having a busy morning, I see,' Florrie said, pointing to the bakery across the street. A bus was parked outside, and people were streaming out from the shop's door, their arms full.

Tindley's bakery was famous for miles. It had almost single-handedly put the little country town back on the map a few years ago, when it had won first prize for the best meat pie in Australia. Travellers and tourists on their way from Sydney to Canberra had begun taking the turn-off from the main highway, just to buy a Tindley pie.

In response to the sudden influx of visitors, the once deserted shops which fronted the narrow and winding main street had thrown open their creaking doors to sell all sorts of arts and crafts.

The area surrounding Tindley had always been a haunt for artists because of its peaceful beauty. But before this new local market had become available they'd had to sell their wares to shopkeepers situated in the more popular tourist towns over on the coast.

Suddenly, it wasn't just pies which attracted visitors, but unique items of pottery and leather goods, wood and home crafts.

In further response to this popularity, even more businesses had opened, offering Devonshire teas and take-away food. Tindley now also boasted a couple of quite good restaurants, and a guest house filled most weekends with Sydney escapees who liked horse-riding and bush walks as well as just sitting on a wide verandah, soaking up the valley views.

Over a period of five years Tindley had been resurrected from being almost a ghost town into a thriving little community with a bustling economy. Enough to support two doctors. Jason had bought into old Doc Brandewilde's general practice five months ago, and hadn't regretted it for a moment.

Admittedly, he'd taken a while to settle to the slower pace after working twelve-hour days in a gung-ho bulk-billing surgery in Sydney. He'd found it difficult at first to resist the automatic impulse to hurry consultations. Old habits did die hard.

Now, he could hardly imagine spending less than fifteen minutes to treat and diagnose a patient. They were no longer nameless faces, but people he knew and liked, people like Florrie, here. Having a warm, friendly chat was a large part of being a family doctor in the country.

The bus started up and slowly moved off, happy faces peering out of the windows.

'I hope Muriel hasn't sold my lunch,' Jason said, and Florrie laughed.

'She'd never do that, Doctor. You're her pet customer. She was saying to me just the other day that if she were thirty years younger, you wouldn't have to put up with Martha's matchmaking, because she'd have snapped you up already.'

Now Jason laughed, though a little drily. Matchmaking wasn't just Martha Brandewilde's domain. All the ladies in Tindley seemed to have got in on the act, his arrival in town causing much speculation among its female population. Apparently, it wasn't often that an attractive unattached bachelor under forty took up residence there. At only thirty, and better looking than average, he was considered ripe and ready for matching.

Not that they'd had any success, despite Jason being invited to several dinner parties where lo and behold, there had just happened to be a spare single girl placed right next to him. Jason suspected he'd been a severe disappointment to his various hostesses so far. Martha Brandewilde was particularly frustrated with him.

Still, he found it reassuring that, despite his apparent lack of enthusiasm for the young ladies served up to him on a platter, there had never been the remotest rumour or suggestion he might be a confirmed bachelor. This was one of the things he found so endearing about Tindley's residents. They held simple old-fashioned views and values.

Florrie gave him a frowning look. 'How old are you, Dr Steel?'

'Thirty, Florrie. Why?'

'A man shouldn't get too old before marrying,' she advised. 'Otherwise he gets too set in his ways. And too selfish. Still, don't be pressured into marrying the wrong girl, now. Marriage is a serious business. But a fine, intelligent man like you knows that. Probably why you're being so choosy. Oh, goodness, look at the time! I must go. *The Midday Show* will have started and I do so hate to miss it.'

Florrie hurried off, leaving Jason to consider what she'd said.

Actually, he agreed with her wholeheartedly. About everything. His life *would* be complete if he could find a good woman to share it with. He might have come to Tindley disillusioned with a certain lady doctor he'd left behind, but his disillusionment hadn't extended to the whole female race. He wanted to marry, but not just anyone.

He shook his head at how close he had come to marrying Adele. What a disaster that would have been!

Admittedly, she'd been a very exciting woman to live with. Beautiful. Brilliant. Sexy as hell. He'd been blindly in love with her, right up till that awful day when the wool had finally fallen from his eyes and he'd suddenly seen the real woman beneath the glittering façade: a coldly unfeeling creature who'd been capable of standing there and dismissing the death of a child with such chilling nonchalance, taking no blame whatsoever for her own negligence, saying that was life and it wouldn't be the last time such an accident happened.

He'd decided to walk away from her then, as well as from his own increasingly selfish and greedy lifestyle. And it had cost him plenty. Rather than fight

Adele in court for his half, he'd given her the place at Palm Beach, and the Mercedes, walking out with little in the way of material possessions. After paying Doc Brandewilde for his half of the practice, Jason had arrived in Tindley with nothing but his clothes, his video collection and a car which was as far from a red Mercedes sports as one could get. White, four-doored and Australian-made. Reliable, but not flashy. The sort of car a country doctor should drive.

Adele had thought him insane, had given him six months to come to his senses. But Jason knew he'd already done that. He wanted no more of the fast life, of the obsessive acquiring of wealth, or even the sort of wild, often kinky sex that women like Adele liked, and demanded. He wanted peace of mind and body. He wanted a family. He wanted marriage to a woman he could respect and like.

Being in love, however, he could do without.

Naturally, he wanted to *want* his wife. Sex was as important to Jason as any other red-blooded man. The town wasn't the only thing being warmed up by spring, and, quite frankly, his celibate lifestyle was beginning to pall. He needed a wife and he needed one soon!

Unfortunately, his chances of marrying the only girl to seriously catch his eye since he'd come to Tindley were less than zero.

He glanced down the road to the small shop on the corner. Its doors were still firmly shut. Understandable, he supposed. Ivy Churchill's funeral had only been last week.

Would Emma stay on and run her aunt's sweet

shop? Jason wondered. Even if she did, where would that get him? Her heart belonged elsewhere, stolen by some local creep who'd done her wrong and left town some time back. According to her aunt, she was still madly in love with this rotter, and probably waiting for him to return.

Jason had been told these scant but dismaying details on his second home visit to the old lady, perhaps because he'd cast one too many admiring glances Emma's way during his first visit.

Not that the girl had noticed herself. She'd seemed oblivious of his admiration as she sat by the window in her aunt's bedroom, doing some of her much admired tapestry work.

It had been impossible, however, not to look at her. Jason's eyes had been drawn again and again to the exquisite picture she'd made, sitting there with her long, slender neck bent in an elegant arc, her eyes downcast, long curling eyelashes resting against her pale cheeks. She'd been wearing a white ankle-length dress with a lacy bodice and a flowing skirt. The setting sun's rays had been shining over her shoulder, turning the soft fair curls hanging around her face into spun gold. A gold chain had hung around her throat, falling slightly away from her skin, swaying with each movement of the large needle she was moving in and out of the canvas.

Jason could still recall how he'd felt as he'd watched her, how he'd ached to slide his hand up and down the delicate curve of her neck, how he'd imagined taking that chain and pulling it gently backwards till her head tipped up and back. In his mind's eye, he'd bent his lips to her startled mouth, before something his patient said had snapped him out of his dream-like, yet highly erotic reverie.

His thoughts had aroused him then. They aroused him now.

Scowling, Jason launched himself across the road and up onto the verandah of the bakery shop. But as he reached to open the shop screen door, he swiftly replaced the scowl with a more pleasant expression.

One minor drawback to life in Tindley was that nothing went unnoticed, not even a passing scowl. He didn't want it getting around town that poor Dr Steel was having personal problems. He also knew not to ask any questions which might be misinterpreted. He was dying to enquire about Emma's intentions, but suspected this might raise a few eyebrows.

'Mornin', Dr Steel,' Muriel chirped straight away on seeing him. 'The usual?'

'Yes, thanks, Muriel.' And he threw her a smile.

By the time he'd selected an orange juice from the self-serve fridge in the corner, his 'usual' of a steak and mushroom pie along with two fresh bread rolls was perched in paper bags on the counter. He was about to pay for it and just go, when curiosity got the better of him.

'I noticed the sweet shop's still closed,' he said, as casually as he could.

Muriel sighed. 'Yes. Emma said she just couldn't face it this week. I feel so sorry for that girl. Her aunt was all she had in this world and now she's gone too. Cancer is a terrible disease. Truly terrible!'

'That it is,' Jason agreed, and handed over a five-dollar note.

Muriel busied herself at the cash register. 'When I go, I'd like to pop off in my sleep with a nice heart attack. Nothing slow and lingering. Frankly, I was surprised Ivy lasted as long as she did. When Doc Brandewilde sent her up to that hospital in Sydney last year for chemotherapy, I wouldn't have given her more than a few days. But she lingered on for over a year. In a way, I suppose it's a relief for Emma that she's finally gone. No one likes to see someone they love in pain. But she's going to be awfully lonely, that girl.'

'I suppose so,' Jason said. 'Er…it's surprising that a pretty girl like Emma doesn't have a boyfriend,' he ventured, trying to look innocent.

Muriel shot him a sharp look. 'Surely you've heard about Emma and Dean Ratchitt. I would have thought Ivy would have said something, what with your visiting her so often these last few months.'

'I don't recall her mentioning anyone by that name,' Jason said truthfully. Dean Ratchitt, eh? The only Ratchitt he knew was Jim Ratchitt, a cranky old so-and-so who lived on a run-down dairy farm just out of town. 'Is he related to Jim Ratchitt?'

'His son. Look, you might as well know the score,' Muriel said as she handed over the change. 'Especially if you're thinkin' of casting your eye in *that* direction.'

'What score do you mean, Muriel?'

Muriel gave him a dry look. 'About Emma and Dean, of course.'

'They were lovers?'

'Oh, I don't know about *that*. Dean liked his girls free and easy, and Emma's not that way at all. Ivy brought her up with solid old-world standards. That girl believes in white weddings and the sanctity of marriage. Still…who knows? Dean had a way with women, there's no doubt about that. And they *were* engaged, however briefly.'

'Engaged!' Ivy hadn't mentioned any engagement.

'Yes. Just before Ivy went up to Sydney last year. Took the town by surprise, I can tell you, since Dean had been squiring another girl around town the month before. Anyway, Emma was sporting his ring just before she went up to Sydney with Ivy. By the time they got back, a couple of months later, it was all over town that Dean had got the youngest Martin girl in trouble.'

'The girl he was seeing before Emma?'

'Oh, no, that was Lizzie Talbot. Anyway, he didn't deny sleeping with the Martin girl, but refused to acknowledge the child, saying the girl was a slut and he wasn't the only bloke who'd been having sex with her. Emma and he had this very public row, right outside Ivy's shop. I heard some of it. Heck, the whole *town* heard some of it!'

Muriel lent on her elbows on the counter, enjoying herself relaying the gossip. 'Dean had the hide to still ask her to marry him, you see. Emma refused and he lost his temper, claimed that everything was her fault, though how he figured that I'd like to know. I remember him yellin' at her that if she didn't marry him as planned, then they were finished. She yelled back that they were finished anyway. She threw his ring back in his face and said she'd marry the first decent man who asked her.'

'*Really?*' Jason said, unable to hide his elation at this last piece of news.

'Don't go countin' your chickens, Doc,' Muriel said drily. 'She was only spoutin' off, like women do. Pride and all. Her actions since then have been much louder than her words. It's been a year and she hasn't gone out on one date, despite being asked many times. No man'll ask her to marry him when she doesn't let them get to first base, will he? We all know she's just waitin' for Dean to show up on her doorstep again. If and when he does...' Muriel shrugged resignedly, as though it was a foregone conclusion that Emma would fall readily into the arms of her long-lost lover.

And he *had* been her lover. Jason didn't doubt that. Women in love were rarely sustained by old-fashioned standards.

Still, the thought of Emma falling victim to such a conscienceless stud churned his stomach. She was such a soft, sweet creature, warm and caring and loving. She deserved better.

She deserves *me*, Jason decided. Modesty had never been one of his virtues.

'What happened to the girl?' he asked. 'The one Ratchitt got into trouble.'

'Oh, she moved away to the city. Rumour has it she got rid of the baby.'

'Do you think it *was* his?'

'Who knows? The girl *was* on the loose side. If it was Dean's child, it's the first time he slipped up that way. Odd, since over the years he'd made out with just about every female under forty in town, married *and* single.'

Jason's eyebrows lifted. 'That's some record. What's he got going for him? Or dare I ask?'

Muriel laughed. 'Can't give a personal report, Doc, since I'm headin' for sixty myself. But he's a right good-lookin' lad, is our Dean.'

'How old is he?'

'Oh, a few years younger than you, I would say, but a few years older than Emma.'

'And how old's Emma?'

Muriel straightened, her expression reproachful. 'Doc, Doc…what have you been doin' these past few months during your home visits? You should know these things already, if you're serious about the girl. She's twenty-two.'

Jason frowned. He'd thought she was older. There was a maturity and serenity in her manner which suggested a few more years' experience in life. Hell, at twenty-two she was barely more than a girl. A girl who'd lived all her life in a country town. An inexperienced and innocent young girl.

Emma's brief engagement to Dean Ratchitt came to mind, and Jason amended that last thought. Not so innocent, perhaps. Nor quite so inexperienced. Men like Ratchitt didn't hang around girls who didn't give them what they wanted.

'Do you think Ratchitt will come back?'

'Who knows? If he hears about Ivy passin' on and Emma inheritin' the shop and all, he might.'

Jason didn't think Emma inheriting that particular

establishment would inspire even the most hard-up scoundrel to race back home. The small shop had provided the two women with a living, he supposed, but only because they didn't have to pay rent. The shop occupied the converted front rooms of an old weatherboard house, as did most of the shops in Tindley. But it was smaller and more run-down than most. As real estate went, it wasn't worth much.

Jason couldn't imagine Ratchitt returning for such a poor prize. But who knew? Those who had nothing…

'If he did come back, do you think she'd take up with him again?' Jason asked.

Muriel pulled a face. 'Love makes fools of the best of us.'

Jason had to agree. Just as well *he* wasn't in love with the girl. He wanted to make his decisions about her with his head, not his heart.

'See you tomorrow, Muriel,' he said, and gathered up his lunch. He'd already tarried far too long in Tindley's bakery. Muriel was going to have a field-day gossiping about what she'd gleaned.

Not that it would matter. Jason had made up his mind, and he would make his move this evening, after afternoon surgery. He had no intention of waiting till the dastardly Dean showed up. He had no intention of wasting time asking Emma for a date, either. He was going to go straight to the heart of the matter…with a proposal of marriage.

CHAPTER TWO

JASON was beginning to feel a bit nervous, a most unusual state for him.

But understandable, he decided as he opened the side gate which led round to the back of Emma's house. It wasn't every day you asked a woman to marry you, certainly not a woman you didn't love, whom you'd never even been out with, let alone slept with. Most people would say he was mad. Adele certainly would.

Thinking of Adele's opinion had a motivating effect on him. Anything Adele thought was insane was probably the most sensible thing in the world.

Determined not to change his mind, Jason closed the gate behind him and strode down the side path to Emma's back door. A light was shining through the lace curtains at the back window, he noted with relief. Some music was on somewhere. She was definitely home.

There were three steps leading up to the back door, the cement worn into dips in the middle. Jason put one foot on the first step, then stopped to straighten his tie and his jacket.

Not that any straightening was strictly necessary. He was wearing one of his suavest and most expensive Italian suits, a silk blend in a dark grey which never creased and always made him feel like a million dollars. His tie was silk too, a matching grey with diagonal stripes of blue and yellow. It was smart and modern without being too loud. He'd even sprayed himself with some of the cologne he was partial to, but kept for special occasions.

Jason knew his mission tonight was a difficult one and he was leaving nothing to chance, using everything in his available armoury to present an attractive and desirable image to Emma. He wanted to be everything he was sure Dean Ratchitt wasn't. He wanted to offer her everything Dean Ratchitt hadn't. A solid, secure marriage to a man who would never be unfaithful to her, and whom she could be proud of.

Taking a deep, steadying breath, he stepped up, lifted his hand and knocked. In the several seconds it took for her to come to the door, a resurgence of nerves set his empty stomach churning. He should have eaten first, he thought irritably. But he hadn't been able to settle to a meal before hearing Emma's answer.

That *she* might think him mad as well suddenly occurred to him, and he was besieged by a most uncustomary lack of confidence.

She'll turn you down, man, came the voice of reason. *She's a romantic and she doesn't love you.*

The door handle slowly turned and the door swung back, sending a rectangle of light right into his face. Emma stood, silhouetted in the doorway, her face in shadow.

'Jason?' came her soft and puzzled enquiry. It had

taken him weeks of visiting Ivy to get her to call him Jason, he recalled. Even then, she still called him Dr Steel occasionally. He was glad she hadn't tonight.

'Hello, Emma,' he returned, amazed at his cool delivery. His heart might be jumping and his stomach doing cartwheels, but he sounded his usual assured self. 'May I come in for a few minutes?'

'Come in?' she repeated, as though she could not make sense of his request. He hadn't been to visit since her aunt's death. He'd attended the funeral, but not the wake, an emergency having called him back to the surgery. She probably thought that their friendship—such as it was—had died with her aunt's death.

'There's something I want to ask you,' he added.

'Oh…oh, all right.' She stepped back and turned into the light.

Jason followed, frowning. She looked more composed than she had the day of the funeral, but still very pale, and far too thin. Her cheeks were sunken in, making her green eyes seem huge. Her dress hung on her, and her hair looked dull, not at all like the shining cap of golden curls which usually framed her delicately pretty face.

It came to him as he glanced around the spotless but bare kitchen that she probably hadn't been eating properly since her aunt's death. The fruit bowl in the centre of the kitchen table was empty, and so was the biscuit jar. Maybe she didn't have much money to spend on food. Funerals and wakes did not come cheap. Had it taken all her spare cash to bury Ivy?

Damn, but he wished he'd thought of that before.

He should not have stayed away. He should have offered some assistance, seen to it she was looking after herself. What kind of doctor was he? What kind of friend? What kind of man?

The kind who thought he could bowl up here out of the blue and ask this grief-stricken young woman to marry him, simply because it suited his needs. He hadn't stopped to really consider *her* needs, had he? He'd arrogantly thought he could fill them, whatever they were.

God, he hadn't changed at all, he realised disgustedly. He was still as greedy and selfish as ever. When would he learn? Would he ever really change? Hell, he hoped so. He really did.

But knowing what he was didn't change his mind about his mission here tonight. He decided he was still a good catch for a girl whose circumstances weren't exactly top drawer.

'I'll get us some coffee, shall I?' she said dully, and without waiting for an answer moved off to fill the electric kettle and plug it in.

It wasn't the first time she'd made him coffee. She'd done the honours every time he'd come to visit Ivy. She already knew he liked his coffee in a mug, white with one sugar, so she didn't have to ask.

Jason closed the back door behind him and sat down at the old Formica-topped table, silently watching her move about the kitchen, seeing again what he'd seen that first time. The unconscious grace of her movements. The elegance of her long neck. The daintiness of her figure.

Once again, he felt the urge to touch her, to stroke that tempting neck, to somehow seduce her to his suddenly quite strong desire, a desire as strong and almost as compelling as he'd once felt for Adele.

Yet she was nothing like Adele, whose dark and very striking beauty had a sophisticated and hard-edged glamour. Adele's long legs and gym-honed body had looked incredibly sexy in those wicked little black suits she wore to work. And what she did for a red lace teddy had to be seen to be believed.

Somehow Jason couldn't see Emma dressed in either red or black, or having the body to carry off the kind of sexy lingerie Adele had been addicted to.

But, for all that, he found the delicacy of her shape incredibly sensual, as he did the feminine free flowing dresses she favoured. He imagined she probably donned long frilly-necked nighties for bed. But he wouldn't mind that. There was something perversely alluring in a woman covering up her body. It gave her a sense of mystery, a touch-me-not quality that was challenging and arousing.

Jason realised he had no idea what Emma might look like naked, other than slender. Her breasts looked adequate in clothing, but who could say what was bra and what was not? Not that he found small breasts a turn-off. He liked tiny, exquisitely formed things.

She was petite in height as well, head and shoulders shorter than his own six feet two, unlike Adele, who in heels matched him inch for inch. To be honest, he rather liked Emma having to tip back her head to look up at him. He liked everything about her. And, whilst he had no doubt now that he was still a selfish man, Jason vowed never to do anything to deliberately hurt her, anything at all.

'Sorry I haven't got any biscuits or cake to offer you,' she apologised as she carried the two mugs over to the table and sat down opposite him. 'I haven't felt like shopping. Or cooking. Or eating, for that matter.'

'But you should eat, Emma,' he couldn't help advising. 'You don't want to get sick, do you?'

A wan smile flitted across her face, as though she didn't think her getting sick was a matter which would overly trouble her at that moment. Jason frowned at the awful thought she might do something silly. She had to be very down and depressed after her aunt's death.

Yet he could not think of the right thing to say. It seemed his newly acquired bedside manner had suddenly deserted him.

They both sat for a few moments, silently sipping their coffee, till Emma put hers down and looked over at him.

'What did you want to ask me?' she said in that same flat, bleak voice. 'Was it something about Aunt Ivy?'

She wasn't really looking at him, he noted. He might have been wearing anything, for all she cared. Her lack of interest in his swanky suit and spruced-up appearance didn't do much for his already waning confidence.

'No,' he replied. 'No, it wasn't about Ivy. It was about you, Emma.'

'Me?'

The soft surprise in her voice and eyes showed she was taken aback by his displaying any personal interest in her at all. But he'd gone too far in his mind to back down now.

'What are you going to do, Emma,' he asked gently, 'now that Ivy's gone?'

She sighed heavily. 'I have no idea.'

'Do you have any other relatives?'

'Some cousins in Queensland. But I don't know them very well. In fact, I haven't seen them for years.'

'You wouldn't want to move away from Tindley, anyway,' he argued. 'All your friends are here.'

And *me*.

'Yes,' she said, and sighed another deep and very weary sigh. 'I suppose I'll open the shop next week, and just…go on as before.'

Go on as before…

Did that mean waste her life waiting for Dean bloody Ratchitt to return? Didn't she know any relationship with him was a dead loss, even if he did come back?

'I see,' Jason said. 'And what about the future, Emma? A pretty girl like you must be planning on marrying one day.'

'Marrying?'

He saw the pain in her face and wanted to kill that bastard. 'You would make some man a wonderful wife, Emma,' he said sincerely.

She flushed and looked down into her coffee. 'I doubt that,' she muttered.

'Then don't. I think any man you agreed to marry would have to be very lucky indeed.'

His words sent her head jerking up, and Jason saw the dawning of understanding over his visit. Shock filled her eyes.

'Yes,' he said before his courage failed him. 'Yes, Emma, I'm asking you to marry me.'

Gradually, her shock gave way to confusion and curiosity. Her eyes searched his face, looking for God knew what.

'But why?' she said at last.

He should have expected such a question, but it threw him for a moment. *Don't lie,* his conscience insisted.

'Why?' he stalled.

'Yes, why?' she insisted. 'And please don't say you're in love with me, because we both know you're not.'

Jason was tempted to lie. He knew he could be very convincing if he tried. He could say he'd hidden his feelings because Ivy had warned him off. He could say a whole load of conning garbage. But that was not what he wanted. If and when he married Emma, he wanted no lies. No pretence. From either of them.

'No,' Jason replied with a degree of regret in his voice. 'No, I'm not in love with you, Emma. But believe me when I say I find you very pretty and very desirable. I have right from the first time I saw you.'

He took some comfort from the colour which zoomed into her cheeks. Had she been aware of his admiration all along? If she had, she'd never given him any indication, although, to be fair, she'd always been prepared to spend time with him after he'd visited her aunt, always offered him coffee and conversation.

'A man like you could have any girl he wanted,' she countered. 'Ones far prettier and more desirable than me. There's not a single girl in the district who wouldn't throw herself at your feet, if you turned your eye her way.'

But not you, it seems, Jason thought. Damn, but this was not going to be one of his greatest moments. Failure was always a bitter taste in his mouth. In the past, there hadn't been a girl he'd fancied whom he hadn't been successful with.

Keeping his voice steady and calm, and his eyes firmly on hers, he went on. 'I don't want any other girl in the district, Emma. I want you.'

Now she flushed fiercely, and his confidence began to return.

'As I've already said, Emma, I think you'd make a wonderful wife. And a wonderful mother. I watched you with your aunt. You're so kind and caring. So patient and gentle. In the weeks I've known you, I've come to like you very very much. I thought you liked me in return. Was I mistaken?'

'No,' she returned, although warily. 'I *do* like you. But just liking someone is not enough for marriage. Neither is finding them attractive.'

So she found him attractive, did she? That was good. That was very good.

'You think you have to be in love?' he probed softly.

'Well, yes, I do.'

'Six months ago I might have agreed with you,' he said ruefully, and her eyes narrowed on him.

'What do you mean? What happened six months ago?'

Jason hesitated, then gambled on telling her the complete truth. There was a bond in revealing one's soul to another. And one's secrets. He wanted no secrets between them, not if they were to be man and wife. And, by God, they would be, if he had anything to do about it.

'Six months ago I was working with and living with a woman in Sydney. A doctor. I was madly in love with her and we were planning to be married this year. One day, one of her patients died. A little boy. Of bacterial meningitis.'

'Oh, how sad! She must have been very upset.'

'One might reasonably have thought so,' he said bitterly. 'I have no doubt you would have been devastated in her position. But not Adele. Oh, no. The child's death meant nothing to her, other than a slight blow to her ego. She was briefly annoyed she hadn't matched the child's symptoms with the cause, but then how could she, in a mere five minutes' consultation?'

'Five minutes?' She was shocked, he could see.

'That was the average length of a consultation in our surgery. Get 'em in and get 'em out as quickly as possible. Turn-over meant money, you see, and money was the name of the game. Not people. Or lives. Just money.'

She was staring at him, perhaps seeing the truth behind that vitriol, that it wasn't just Adele who'd been greedy and heartless in those days. He'd been just as bad.

He sighed. 'Yes, it's true. There, but for the grace of God, go I.'

'Oh, no, Jason,' she said softly. 'Not you. You're not like that at all. I watched you with Aunt Ivy. You're a very caring man, and a very good doctor.'

His heart squeezed tight. 'You flatter me, Emma. But I would like to think I finally saw the error of my ways and made changes for the better. That's why I left the city and came here, to find my self-respect again, and to find a better way of life.'

'What about your relationship with this Adele?' she asked, her expression thoughtful.

'I could hardly continue to love a woman I despised,' he said.

Her laugh startled him. 'Do you think love is finished as easily as that? Do you think finding out something unpleasant—or even wicked—about the person you love, smashes that love to smithereens? Believe me, Jason, it doesn't.'

Her words were like a kick to his stomach. She still loved Dean Ratchitt, regardless of his faithless character. And she believed he still loved Adele.

Jason tried to give that concept some honest thought. Perhaps he *did* still love her. He certainly thought about her a lot. And he missed her, especially in bed.

But neither of these factors would deter his resolve for a future between himself and Emma. Nor would he let her think he wasn't aware of her unrequited passion for another man.

'I've heard all about Dean Ratchitt,' he said abruptly, and her green eyes flared wide with shock.

'Who from? Aunt Ivy?'

'Amongst others.'

'And what…what did they say?'

'The truth. That you were engaged to be married and he betrayed you with another girl. That you argued and told him you would marry the next man who asked you.' He set steady eyes upon her own stunned gaze. 'So I'm the next man, Emma, and I'm asking you. Marry me.'

Jason was taken aback when her shock swiftly became anger. 'They had no right to tell you that,' she shot back at him. 'I didn't mean it. I *never* meant it. I can't marry you, Jason. I'm sorry.' And she tore her eyes away from his to smoulder down into her coffee.

Her passionate outburst stripped away the cool, calm façade Jason had been hiding behind. He was never at his best when his will was thwarted, especially when he believed what he wanted was for the best for everyone all round.

'Why not?' he demanded to know. 'Because you're waiting for Ratchitt to return?'

'Dean,' she snapped, glittering green eyes flying back to his. 'His name is Dean.'

'Ratchitt matches his character better.'

Her gaze grew distressed and dropped back down. 'He…he might come back,' she mumbled. 'Now that I'm alone, and…and…'

'An heiress?' he supplied for her cuttingly. 'I don't think this place will bring him running, Emma.' And he waved around the ancient and shabbily furnished room. 'Men like Ratchitt want more out of life than some old house in a country backwater, even if the front rooms have been turned into a sweet shop.'

She was shaking her head at him. 'You don't understand.'

'I think I understand the situation very well. He stole your heart, then broke it, without a second thought. I've met men like him before. They can't keep their pants zipped for more than a day, and they love no one but themselves. He's not worth loving, any more than Adele was. I've consigned her to my past. The best thing you can do is consign Ratchitt to your past, and go forward.

'Marry me, Emma,' he urged, when her eyes became confused. 'I promise to be a good husband to you and a good father to our children. You do want children, don't you? You don't want to wake up one day and find that you're a dried-up old spinster with nothing to look forward to but loneliness and rheumatism.'

She buried her face in her hands then, and began to cry. Not noisily, but deeply, her shoulders shaking. Jason was moved as he'd never been moved before. He raced round the table to squat down beside her chair. He reached out to take her small, slender hands in his and turned her tear-stained face towards him.

'I won't hurt you like he did, Emma,' he promised her with a fierce tenderness. 'I give you my word.'

'But it's too soon,' she choked out.

Jason wasn't sure what she meant. 'Too soon?' he probed. 'You mean since Ivy's death?'

'Yes.'

'Are you saying you might marry me later on?'

Her eyes lifted, betraying a haunted, hunted look. She was tempted to say yes, he could see. But something was stopping her.

'A month,' she blurted out. 'Give me a month. Then ask me again.'

Jason sat back on his heels and exhaled slowly, his surge of elation dampened by a prickle of apprehension. It wasn't a long time, a month. But it worried him. He didn't believe the wait had anything to do with Ivy's death. It was all to do with Ratchitt. She still hoped he'd come back for her.

The possibility of that scum showing up again was slight, Jason believed. But even that slight possibility sickened him. The thought of Emma falling back into his filthy arms sickened him even further.

And it did something else. It sparked a jealousy which startled him.

He'd never been a jealous man before. Not even with Adele. Emma was evoking emotions in him that were alien to all his previous experiences with women. Along with the jealousy, he also felt fiercely protective.

Still, he would imagine most men would feel protective of a girl like Emma. She was so fragile-looking. And so sweet. Someone had to stand between her and the Ratchitts of this world. She wasn't experienced enough to see just how bad his type were. How depraved and conscienceless.

'All right, Emma,' Jason agreed. 'A month. But that doesn't mean I can't see you during that month, does it? I'd like to take you out on a regular basis. We could get to know each other better.'

'But…but everyone with think that…that…'

'That you're dating Dr Steel,' he finished firmly. 'What's wrong with that? You're single. I'm single. Single people date each other, Emma. That's hardly grounds for gossip.'

Her eyes almost smiled through their wet lashes. 'You don't know the good ladies of Tindley.'

'Believe me, I'm beginning to. So what about dinner tomorrow night? It's Friday, and I always eat out on a Friday. We could drive over to the coast if you don't want to be seen with me here in Tindley for a while.'

She blinked the last of her tears away and looked at him with that searching gaze he found quite discomfiting. 'Are you going to try to get me into bed afterwards?'

Jason had trouble stopping the guilt from jumping into his eyes. Not that he'd had seduction on the menu for tomorrow night. He'd actually been going to leave that course of action for a week or two.

'No,' he said, with what he hoped was honest-sounding conviction. 'No. I wouldn't do that.'

She looked at him with frowning eyes. 'Why not?' she posed in a puzzled tone. 'You said you found me pretty and desirable. You also asked me to marry you. I imagined you fancied me, at least a little.'

'I *do* fancy you. And more than a little. Hell, Emma.' He stood up and raked his hands back through his hair. She'd thrown him for a loop by being so sexually direct. He hadn't expected it from her. Did she *want* him to try to seduce her or not?

'It's perfectly all right, Jason,' she said calmly. 'I've been brought up in a country town, not a convent. I'm well acquainted with the way men think and feel when it comes to sex. I know you haven't had a girlfriend since coming here to Tindley, and I'm sure you're fairly frustrated by now. I just didn't want to give you false hopes if I agreed to go out to dinner with you. You're a very attractive, experienced man, and I'm sure you know how to get to a girl. But I have no intention of sleeping with you. Not this side of a wedding ring, anyway.'

He stared at her, and her chin tipped up, revealing a side to Emma he hadn't seen before. A very stubborn side. A decidedly steely light gleamed in her green eyes and her attitude was definitely defiant.

One part of him admired her strong old-world standards, till he remembered Ratchitt. He'd bet London to a brick on that she hadn't given *him* the same ultimatum.

Or had she? he suddenly revised. Was that what

had happened between them? Had she refused to sleep with Ratchitt till he'd walked with her to the altar? Had he given her an engagement ring, then simply had other girls on the side till the prize would finally be his without any more arguing, for ever and ever?

'Do you want to take back your proposal now?' she asked challengingly. 'And your dinner invitation?'

'No,' he said slowly. 'But I would like an answer to one simple question.'

'What question's that?'

'Are you a virgin, Emma?'

CHAPTER THREE

THE following day felt interminable to Jason. Several times his mind wandered to that moment the evening before when Emma had looked him straight in the eye and told him the truth. Yes, she was a virgin. So what? Did he have a problem with that?

Did he have a problem with that?

Yes, and no.

Virginity wasn't something he'd encountered before in his personal life. Not once. Adele hadn't been a virgin. Not by a long shot. None of his other girlfriends over the years had been virgins, either.

The thought of making love to a virgin was a little daunting. Unknown territory usually was.

At the same time, the thought of making love to an untouched Emma on their wedding night appealed to a part of him he'd never known existed. He'd never thought of himself as a romantic before. But with Emma he was a different man. He recognised that already. She brought out the best in him.

And perhaps the worst.

Possessiveness and jealousy in men weren't traits he'd ever admired. He didn't like the way such men treated their girlfriends and wives. The females in their lives were flattered for a while—seeing their partners' passion as evidence of the extent of their love. Till reality set in and the flattery gave way to fear. He vowed to fight the temptation to be like that with Emma. He wanted her to be happy as his wife, never afraid.

And she *would* be his wife. He felt confident of that now. It was just a matter of time.

Time…

Jason glanced up at the clock on the wall. Five o'clock. And the small waiting room was still full of wheezing, sneezing patients. The beautiful spring weather had brought a rash of hay-fever sufferers, along with the blossoms.

Sighing, Jason rose from his desk and went to call in the next patient.

'I hope to heaven that's it, Nancy?' Jason said at long last, popping his head around the consulting-room door and sighing with relief when he spied the empty waiting room. The clock on the wall now said five to seven. Surgery usually finished around five-thirty and, whilst it sometimes ran late, it was rarely this late.

'Yes, all finished for the day, Dr Steel,' Nancy returned, in a sighing tone which Jason knew didn't denote tiredness, but a reluctance to leave the love of her life and go home to an empty house.

Not him. The practice!

Nancy had been Doc Brandewilde's resident receptionist - cum - secretary - cum - book - keeper - cum-emergency nurse for the past twenty years. She worked six days a week—seven, if and when required—and overtime without ever asking for an extra cent. Rising sixty now, she was as healthy as a horse and would probably be presiding over the practice for another twenty years at least.

She'd been a bit pernickety with Jason when he'd first arrived, till he'd discovered through Muriel that Nancy was afraid he'd fire her, if and when Doc retired, and Jason took on a new partner. Once Jason had reassured Nancy the job was hers for as long as she wanted it, their relationship had improved in leaps and bounds, although there'd been a temporary hiccup when Jason had suggested they get a computer system for the files and the accounts. He'd made the mistake of saying a computer would be more efficient and cut down on her workload. He hadn't realised, at that point in time, that Nancy didn't *want* to cut down on her workload.

Nancy had gone into an instant panic, then flounced home in a right snip, saying if Jason thought a machine could do a better job than twenty years' experience, then she didn't want to work for such a fool. After one day's mayhem in the surgery, Jason had gone crawling on his hands and knees, begging for her to return. He'd grovelled very well, calling himself an idiot from the city who didn't understand the workings of a country practice, saying if she could be gracious enough to forgive his ignorance and help him wherever possible, he was sure to get the hang of things in due time.

After that, they got on like a house on fire, even though Nancy maintained an old-fashioned formality in addressing him as Dr Steel all the time, which sometimes irritated Jason. Still, that seemed to be the way with people in country towns. They held their doctors in high esteem. Put them on a pedestal, so to speak. And while that was rather nice, Jason sometimes felt a bit of a fraud. If they knew his original motives for choosing medicine as a profession, they might not be so respectful.

'Sorry to love you and leave you, Nancy,' he said briskly, when it became clear she was going to linger, 'but I have to go upstairs and change.'

'Going out for dinner, Doctor?'

'Yes, that's right.'

'Where are you off to tonight?

'I thought I might drive over to the coast.'

'Seems a long way to go to eat alone,' Nancy returned on a dry note.

Jason opened his mouth to lie, but then decided against it. The people of Tindley would like nothing better than to see their second and much younger doctor safely married to a local girl. Doctors were as scarce as hen's teeth in some rural areas. They would exert a subtle—or perhaps *not* so subtle—pressure on Emma, to be a sensible girl and snap up the good doctor while she had the chance.

'Actually, no, I'm not going alone,' he said casually. 'I'm taking Emma Churchill.'

If he'd been expecting shock on Nancy's face, then he was sorely disappointed. Her smile was quite smug. 'I suspected as much.'

'You sus—' Jason broke off, grimacing resignedly. The small town grapevine never ceased to amaze him. 'How on earth did you know?' he asked, with wry acceptance and a measure of curiosity. No way would Emma have told anyone.

'Muriel said you were asking about Emma yester-day. Then Sheryl spotted you going through Ivy's side gate last night. Then Emma dropped in to Beryl's Boutique at lunch-time and bought a pretty new dress. On top of that, you've been clock-watching and jumpy all day. It didn't take too much to put two and two together.'

Jason had to smile. Jumpy, was he? You could say that again. He'd hardly slept a wink last night for thinking about Emma.

'And what will the good ladies of Tindley think about such goings-on?' he asked, still smiling.

Nancy laughed. 'Oh, there won't be any goings-on where Emma is concerned, Dr Steel, so you can save your energy and keep your mind above your trouser belt till the ring's on her finger. You *are* planning on proposing, aren't you?'

Jason saw no point in being coy. 'I am…but that's doesn't mean she'll say yes.'

'She will, if she's got any sense in her head. But there again—' She broke off suddenly, and frowned.

'If you're thinking about Dean Ratchitt, then I know all about him,' he said brusquely. 'Muriel filled me in.'

Nancy's expression was troubled. 'He's bad news, that one. Emma was really stuck on him. Always was, right from her schooldays.'

'I hear he's very handsome.'

Nancy frowned. 'Not handsome, exactly,' she said. Not like you, Dr Steel. Now, you're handsome in my book. But he has something, has Dean. And he has a way about him with the women, no doubt about that.'

'So everyone keeps telling me,' Jason said testily.
'But he's not here in Tindley, Nancy, and I am. So
let's leave it at that, shall we? Now, I must shake a
leg or I'm going to be late.'

'What time did you say you'd pick Emma up?'

'Seven-thirty.'

'Just as well she lives down the road, then, isn't it?
Off you go. I'll lock up here.'

Jason dashed up the stairs, stripping as he went.

Like Ivy's sweet shop, the surgery was part of an
old house which fronted the main street of Tindley.
But where Ivy's place was small and one-storeyed,
the house Doc Brandewilde had bought thirty years
before was two-storeyed and quite spacious. Doc and
his wife had raised three boys in it.

But they'd always wanted a small acreage out of
town, it seemed, and once Jason had expressed interest in the practice Doc had bought his dream place
and moved, leaving the living quarters of the house
in town to his new partner.

Jason had been thrilled. He'd liked the house on
sight. It had character, like those American houses
he'd often seen in movies and which he'd always cov-
eted. Made of wood, it had an L-shaped front verandah, with wisteria wound through the latticed panels,
and a huge front door with a brass knocker and
stained glass panels on either side. Inside, the ceilings
were ten feet high, and all the floors polished wood.
A wide central hall downstairs separated two rooms
on the left and two on the right. It passed a powder
room under the stairs, and led into a large kitchen
which opened out onto a long, wide back verandah.

The two rooms on the left—which had once been the front parlour and morning room—had been converted into the waiting room and surgery. The two on the right remained the dining and lounge rooms.

Upstairs, there had been four bedrooms and one bathroom till a few years back, when Doc's wife, Martha, had brought in the renovators and combined the two smallest bedrooms on the right into a roomy master bedroom and *en suite* bathroom.

Jason rushed into this bathroom now, snapping on the shower and reaching for the soap. No time to shave, he realised. Pity. He'd wanted to be perfect for Emma. Still, he wasn't one of those dark shaven men who grew half a beard by five o'clock in the afternoon. His father had been dark—according to his parents' wedding photos. But his mother fair. He'd ended up being a mixture of both, with mid-brown hair, his father's olive skin and his mother's light blue eyes.

And a blessed lack of body hair, he thought as he lathered up his largely hairless chest.

With time ticking away, he didn't shampoo his hair. No way did he want to front up with wet hair. Snapping off the taps, he dived out of the shower, grabbed a towel and began to rub vigorously. Five minutes later he was standing in his underpants, scanning his rather extensive wardrobe.

No suit tonight, he thought. Tonight called for something a little less formal, which didn't really present a problem, except in making a choice. During his days as a dashing young Sydney doctor, he'd bought clothes for every occasion.

His eyes moved up and down the hangers several

times. Damn, but he had too many clothes! Finally, he grabbed the nearest hanger to his hand, and had already dragged on the cream trousers, pale blue silk shirt and navy blazer before remembering Adele had chosen that very outfit the last time they'd gone shopping together. She'd said it made him look like a millionaire, fresh from winning the Sydney to Hobart yacht race. She'd liked the image, said it turned her on. Nothing turned Adele on, Jason thought ruefully, like the thought of money.

He scowled at the memory, but had no time to change, consoling himself with the thought that at least the woman had had taste in men's clothes.

She came to mind again as he slipped on the sleek gold watch and the onyx dress ring he always wore. Both had been presents from Adele, bought in the first year of their three together. She'd given him quite a few personal gifts in those early days, mostly to enhance his new status as her partner.

Jason felt no personal attachment for the gifts any more. Usually he wore them without a second thought. But it didn't seem right to wear them when he was going out with the woman he was going to marry. He compromised by leaving the ring off but wearing the watch, because he liked knowing the time. Still, he determined to buy himself another watch in the morning. Something less flashy.

Scooping up his wallet and car keys, he turned and went forth to make his destiny.

Emma was ready and waiting for him, as pretty as a picture in a dress just made for her pale colouring and willowy slenderness. Round-necked and long-sleeved, it was mainly cream, but tie-dyed with splashes of peach and the palest orange. The material was light and crinkly, the style on the loose side, skimming over the gentle rise of her bust and falling in soft folds to her ankles. Her fair curly hair had obviously been shampooed and especially conditioned, for it shone in contrast to the previous night's dullness. Her face had some colour too—thanks to some lipstick and blusher, perhaps? Her eyes looked huge, even though he could see no visible make-up around them. When her neck craned back to look up at him, a faint smell of lavender wafted from her skin.

She looked like something from another world. A unique treasure to be cherished and cared for.

Was that how Ratchitt had seen her when he'd pursued her? Or was Emma just another notch on his belt? Had her purity enraged or enslaved him? Jason couldn't see the rotter who'd been described to him as having any sensitivity. He'd probably only asked Emma to marry him because he thought she'd come across once a ring was on her finger.

Jason was glad he'd failed to get what he wanted. He didn't deserve her. Men like him didn't deserve any decent woman, let alone *his* Emma.

And that was how he saw her now. *His* Emma.

'You look lovely,' he said, his eyes raking over her with what he hoped wasn't too impassioned a gaze. But, dear heaven, he *did* desire her. Yet so differently from the way he'd desired Adele.

Adele, he'd wanted to ravage. With her, he'd wanted to take, never to give. After all, Adele was one of those liberated females who shouted to the

rooftops that they were responsible for their own or-
gasms, and she *had* been, at times. He and Adele
hadn't made love, he now saw. They'd had sex. Great
sex, it was true. But still just sex, the only aim being
mutual physical satisfaction.

Emma made him want to give. Jason had no doubt
that his priority when he made love to her would be
to give her the most wonderful experience in her life,
an experience which would banish Ratchitt from her
mind for ever. His own pleasure would be second-
ary…which was an extraordinary first for him when
it came to sex. Maybe he *had* changed, after all!

'You look very nice yourself,' she was saying.
'Very…handsome.'

At least she hadn't said rich.

'Thank you. Shall we go? My car's out in the street.
There again,' he added, smiling a wry smile, 'my
car's always parked out in the street.'

That was one thing his new house didn't have. A
garage. There was room in the back yard, but no ac-
cess down the side.

You can't have everything in life, son…

Jason glanced over at Emma, and his smile softened.

Maybe not, Mum. But I'm getting closer.

CHAPTER FOUR

'WHAT happened to your ring?'

Jason was about to fork a honeyed prawn into his mouth when Emma posed the unexpected query. Slowly, he lowered his fork to the plate, and looked across the table into her big, luminous green eyes.

Her asking such a question was telling, he thought, for it revealed she'd noticed his always wearing the ring in the first place. He reasoned that you wouldn't notice such a thing—or its absence—if you hadn't been watching a person fairly closely.

The thought flattered his ego.

He was also grateful that their conversation had finally become a little more personal. During the drive over to Bateman's Bay, Emma had been quiet and tense. Jason had had the awful feeling she was regretting coming with him, regretting having anything to do with him at all. Sensing her mood, he hadn't pressed her with any questions of his own, keeping the conversation light and inconsequential. He'd tried amusing her with an account of his relationship with Nancy so far, but, whilst she'd laughed at the right moments, he'd suspected her mind was elsewhere. Ratchitt, probably.

Now he wasn't so sure. Her eyes were focused on *his* face with a concentration which was total and exclusive. He almost preened under the triumphant and very male feelings her intense gaze evoked.

'I took it off,' he said. 'And left it off.'

'But why?' she asked, perplexed. 'It was a beautiful ring.'

'Adele gave it to me.'

'Oh,' she murmured, and looked down at her largely untouched Mongolian lamb.

'She gave me this watch too,' he added matter-of-factly. 'And it's going to be replaced in the morning as well.'

Her eyes lifted, confusion in their depths. 'You sound so calm about it.'

'I *am* calm about it. They have no meaning for me any more. I don't want anything of hers around me,' he finished with a betraying burst of emotion.

Her smile was rueful. 'You still love her.'

'Maybe. But I certainly won't for ever. Time cures all wounds, Emma.'

'That's a simplistic statement for a doctor to make, Jason. Time doesn't always cure. Some wounds fester further. Some become ulcers. Some turn into gangrene, and ultimately kill.'

There was a moment's stark silence between them. Jason was horrified at the depth of her pain over that creep. God, how she must have loved him! Was he foolish in thinking she would ever get over him, that they could be happy together? Was his ego overriding reality?

'What are you going to do with them?' she asked abruptly. 'The ring and the watch.'

'I'll post them to one of my brothers. Jerry, I think. He'll love them.'

'One of your brothers,' she repeated slowly, and shook her head. 'I'd forgotten you would have a family somewhere. I'm used to being alone, you see. I forget other people have parents and brothers and sisters.'

'Actually, I don't have any parents any more. My mother's dead and my father's God knows where. He ran out on Mum the year I was born. I don't have any sisters, either, but I do have five older brothers. I had six till Jack was killed in a motorbike accident, which leaves James, Josh, Jake, Jude and Jerry, working from the eldest down. I'm the youngest. Mum liked boy's names starting with J, as you can see.'

She smiled at that. 'And where are they, your brothers? What are they doing?'

'Scattered to the four corners of the earth. Since Mum died we don't keep in touch much. Typical boys, I guess. But Jerry's closest to me in age and I have a soft spot for him. He's not too bright, works in a clothing factory in Sydney and doesn't earn much. He's not married and lives in a boarding house. I send him some money sometimes. And clothes and things.' Actually he hadn't sent Jerry anything for ages, not since his break-up with Adele. His mind had been elsewhere. He vowed to do something about that, come Monday.

'I would have liked a big brother,' she said wistfully. 'But I was an only child. My parents were getting on when they had me. Aunt Ivy was my Dad's sister.'

'Ivy mentioned your parents were killed in a helicopter crash.'

'Yes. A joy flight. Ironic term, don't you think?'

'Tragic.'

'We were holidaying at this resort on the Gold Coast. I was ten. I was going to go up in the helicopter with them, but I'd eaten too much rubbish earlier, which hadn't agreed with me, and they left me behind because they thought I might be sick all over them. I actually saw the helicopter crash. It clipped the top of a tree as it was taking off and just tipped head-first into the ground.'

'What a dreadful thing for you to witness,' he sympathised.

'It was, I suppose. But, to be honest, I wasn't as devastated at some children might have been. I never felt my parents really loved me. I was an unwanted pregnancy, you see. Totally unexpected. Mum often said to Dad in my presence that they were too old to have a child, that I was a nuisance and she should have had an abortion.'

Jason didn't know what to say to that. He'd never felt his father's rejection because his father had never been around. To be constantly told you weren't wanted must have been awful. And not too good for your self-esteem. He might have been dirt-poor, but he'd always known he'd been the apple of his mother's eye.

'Anyway, when Aunt Ivy took me in,' Emma went on, 'I finally knew what it was to be loved and wanted. She was so good to me. So very, very good...'

Tears welled up in her eyes, but she staunchly blinked them away and wiped her eyes with the red serviette from her lap. 'Sorry,' she muttered, scrunching up the serviette and lowering it to her lap again. 'I promised myself I would be good company for you tonight. But I haven't been, have I? I won't blame you if you never ask me out again, let alone ask me to marry you again.'

He stared at her. What was that odd note in her voice? Had she had second thoughts since refusing him last night? Had she decided she was a fool to wait any longer for Ratchitt's return?

'I wouldn't worry about that, if I were you, Emma,' Jason said. 'I *will* ask you out again. And I *will* ask you to marry me again. Again *and* again. I intend asking you till the answer is yes.'

Her intake of breath was deep, but she let it out slowly. Her eyes never left his, as though she could plumb the depths of his soul if she looked long enough and hard enough. 'You're very strong-minded, aren't you?' she said.

'I know what I want. And I want you, Emma.'

Her face twisted into a tight grimace and he thought she might cry again. But she didn't. 'I…I don't think I'd make you a wonderful wife at all,' she said in a wretched voice.

'Why's that?'

'I… I…' She shook her head again and fell silent, her eyes dropping. But not before Jason glimpsed something that looked like guilt.

'Tell me why, Emma?' he demanded to know. If there was one thing he could not stand, it was being

kept in the dark about something. He always needed
to know the truth, no matter how unpalatable. He
could cope with the truth. What he could not cope
with was deception and evasion.

'Emma, look at me,' he ordered, and she obeyed,
however reluctantly. 'Now, tell me why you said that.
And be honest. Don't be afraid. Nothing you say will
shock me, or make me angry.'

'You won't want to hear *this*.'

'Try me, Emma.'

She remained silent.

'*Trust* me.'

'Even if I agree to marry you,' she confessed on a
whisper, 'I know I'll never forget Dean. And I'll
never love *you* while Dean's here in my heart, no
matter how much I might want to.'

Jason sucked in a sharp breath. He had guessed that
was what might be troubling her. But still…hearing
her say the words hurt far more than he could ever
have imagined. He supposed at the back of his mind
he'd hoped that eventually she would learn to love
him, as he was sure he would learn to love her. He
might still be in love with Adele at the moment, but
he believed time would definitely cure *that* particular
wound.

Time…

Of course! That was the crux of all his problems
with Emma, he realised on a wave of relief. Time.

She might believe with all her heart in what she
was saying, but that was now, this very minute, tonight, not tomorrow, or next month, or next year.
Young love could be very intense, but young love,

like a young plant, didn't survive indefinitely without being fed and watered. In the end it withered and died.

When Ratchitt didn't come back, Emma's love for him would wither and die as well, replaced by a new love, for her husband. Emma was too sweet and caring a person to deny affection if he was kind and attentive to her.

When she placed her crumpled serviette beside her plate on the table, he reached across and took her hand in his. She immediately stiffened under his touch, but he persisted, stroking the length of her fingers with gentle fingertips. 'You let me worry about what kind of wife you'll be to me,' he said softly. 'It's my job to make you happy, Emma. I think I can do that. In fact, I—'

He was startled when she snatched her hand away and put it back in her lap. 'I don't want you touching me like that,' she snapped, but would not look at him. There was a high colour in her cheeks which he found encouraging.

'I'm sorry,' he said, though he wasn't sorry at all.

Perhaps his lack of sincerity echoed in his voice, for her eyes swung back to glower at him. 'Don't ever say sorry to me when you're not! And don't ever, *ever* say you love me when you don't!'

He was stunned by her attack. He hadn't known she had that kind of spirit. Or such a temper!

'All right,' he agreed, still a bit shell-shocked.

Her fierce expression suddenly sagged, as did her shoulders. 'I'm sorry,' she said. 'I'm being a right bitch.'

He almost smiled. She had no idea what a 'right

bitch' was really like. Adele would eat her for break-fast.

'Why don't we stop apologising to each other,' he said, 'and eat up our dinner? You said you liked Chinese, remember? That's why we came here, and not that nice little Italian restaurant down the road.'

'I should have let you have your way,' she said as she toyed with her meal. 'I don't have much of an appetite lately. Do you like Italian food an awful lot?'

'Love it. But I also like Chinese, as well as German, French, Asian, Thai and Japanese. Fact is, I like food, period. As long as I don't have to cook it.'

'Normally, I love to cook,' she said.

'That's good.'

Her glance was sharp. 'I haven't said I'm going to marry you yet, Jason,' she reprimanded rather primly.

'I can live in hope, can't I?'

Her face clouded. 'They might be false hopes.'

'I'm willing to risk it.'

She stiffened in her chair. 'You don't think he'll ever come back, do you?'

'If he loved you, nothing would have kept him away. There again, if he loved you, he would not have done what he did in the first place.'

'You're so black and white,' she said, and sighed. 'I know what Dean did was wrong. And I can't con-done it. But I also know he loved me. That's what makes everything so hard. Knowing that.'

'I see.' And he did.

When he'd told Adele he was leaving her, she'd been angrier than he'd ever seen her. How could he leave her when they loved each other so much? When

she loved *him* so much? She'd tried everything to persuade him differently. She'd appealed to every weak-
ness she thought he had. His ambition. His greed. His
supposed love of city life.

And sex, of course. She'd thrown everything at him
in that regard, tried everything, done everything.

And he'd let her, to his discredit. But he'd still
walked away in the end. No, he'd run, before she
could persuade him differently.

What would he have done, he wondered now, if
she'd come after him? If she'd shown up during his
first few weeks here in Tindley, when he'd thought
he'd made the biggest mistake in his life, before he'd
got used to the slower pace, before the town and the
people and the peace and quiet had seeped into his
soul.

Maybe—just maybe—he'd have allowed himself to
be seduced back to Sydney, despite his better judgement.

So he *did* understand how Emma felt.

But people like Adele and Ratchitt didn't love as
deeply or as long as others. Adele hadn't run after
him, and Ratchitt had not come back.

He looked at Emma's depressed face and decided
a change of subject was called for.

'Do you want dessert, perhaps?' he asked. 'I can
see you're not going to eat that. But something sweet
usually goes down easily.'

'All right,' she agreed, brightening. 'I wouldn't
mind some ice-cream.'

'Is that all?'

'Yes, but with lots of flavouring.'

'Your wish is my command.' And he signalled the waitress.

He kept the conversation off lost loves for the rest of the night, and the drive back to Tindley was much more relaxed than the drive over. He regaled her with tales of his days at university, including some of the jobs he'd done to pay his way through.

By the time he eased his car into the kerb outside the sweet shop, Emma was laughing. 'You really worked in a gay bar?'

'For one evening only,' he returned drily as he switched off the engine and unclicked his seat belt. 'I didn't know it was a gay bar when I applied. I was walking past and saw a sign in the window saying 'Drinks Waiter Wanted'. I went right in and was hired on the spot.'

'When did the penny drop?'

'I realised my mistake pretty quickly that night, but I decided I could cope when I saw the size of my tips.'

'And?'

'I lasted three hours before I admitted defeat and quit. It seemed I wasn't as money-hungry as I'd thought I was. I had to leave, or end up in jail. Because, believe me, if one more guy had squeezed my buns as I walked past, I was going to give him a mouthful of fist.'

'Oh, that's so funny! Still, I'll bet you were a very cute young man.'

'Cute!' God, but he hated that word.

She laughed some more, her mouth falling open and her eyes dancing over at him.

He didn't mean to do it. He really didn't. But she was so lovely and he'd been so lonely. Before he knew it he was twisting in his seat, leaning over the gear lever, cupping her face and kissing her.

She didn't resist him, despite the firm pressure of his mouth on hers, despite his tongue taking advantage of her parted lips, despite all those old-world values of hers.

Oh, yes, there *was* a fleeting moment when she froze beneath his kiss, and her hands *did* flutter up from her lap to lie, palms flat, against his chest. But she didn't press him away, or try to shut her mouth. She accepted the intimate invasion of his tongue, and even moaned a soft moan of pleasure.

It was that soft moan of pleasure which opened the floodgates of his suppressed passion and showed Jason that his notion of always wanting to 'give' when making love to Emma was a fallacy. All of a sudden, giving had nothing to do with his feelings. Seduction became the name of the game. Seduction, and coercion, and possibly corruption. He wanted to make her moan again, wanted to make her forget who she was with, wanted her to surrender blindly to his will.

His mouth ravaged on while his right hand lifted from her face in search of her breasts. He found one through her clothes, warm and soft and surprisingly full. He kneaded it with his fingers, his thumb-pad feeling for, and finding, the nipple. She moaned again, a muffled, choked sound which spoke of a pleasure which both shocked and delighted her. Her back arched away from the seat slightly, pushing her breast more firmly into his highly experienced hand.

Jason became so caught up in her responses—not to mention his own galloping arousal—that he didn't at first feel her pushing against his chest. It wasn't till her struggle turned panicky that he registered she was no longer wanting him to continue.

He'd never encountered resistance to his lovemaking before. Not at this advanced point. It stunned him, when, for a split second, he couldn't—or wouldn't—stop.

But then he did, his mouth wrenching from hers as he slumped back into his seat. His right hand, which moments before had been teasing her nipple into taut erection, lifted to comb his hair back from his sweat-beaded forehead.

'Sorry,' he muttered, furious that he might have just jeopardised his chances with her. But, hell on earth, she could have stopped him sooner.

She didn't say a word, just sat there, staring out of the passenger window with her hands clenched tightly in her lap. He saw that her breathing was still erratic and her cheeks were flaming.

'I said I was sorry, Emma,' he repeated tautly, his own breathing only now calming down. The rest of him wasn't in good shape, either, and promised a sleepless night ahead. Either that, or several cold showers. Any other alternative repulsed him these days. He wasn't a randy adolescent with no self-control. He was a man, a man who wanted a woman, not self-gratification.

Her head slowly turned and her eyes were wide and glazed-looking.

'You don't understand what you've just done,' she said shakily.

'What? What have I done?'

'You've shattered everything I've always believed about myself.'

'Which is?'

'That I would only ever feel like this with Dean...'

'Like what, exactly?'

'Like this...' And, taking his hand, she placed it on her breast again, so that he could feel the still hard nipple, plus the mad pounding of her heart beneath.

The extent of her sexual naivety really hit home. Jason conceded that he could use her lack of experience to bend her to his will—this very night, if he chose. But he knew she would regret it bitterly in the morning. And blame him.

He wanted her respect, as well as her body. Above all, he wanted her as his wife. So it was against his best interests to seduce her. But he wasn't going to let her go on believing his hand on her breast was anything more than it was.

'Love and sex do not have to go hand in hand, Emma,' he murmured as he knowingly and ruthlessly caressed her breast once more, watching in dark triumph as her lips gasped apart. 'What you're feeling is simply a matter of chemistry, and hormones.'

Abruptly, he removed his hand, more for his own benefit at that point than for hers. There was only so much he could take.

'You're a grown woman, Emma,' he said a little harshly, 'and you're probably as frustrated as I am.'

'But I thought that...that...'

'That frustration was a male domain? That nice girls didn't want or need sex?'

'No. Yes. No. I don't know. I…I thought nice girls had to be in love to want to make love.'

'I'm sure being in love would enhance the experience emotionally, but making love without love can still be…extremely satisfying.'

She stared at him, and he could almost read her mind. She was thinking what it might be like to make love with him. She'd enjoyed his kiss, thrilled to his hand on her breast over her clothes. How much more pleasurable to have his hands on both breasts, naked, to have his hands all over her, inside her, to have *him* inside her.

He had difficulty controlling the surge of arousal which threatened to make him throw all caution to the winds. He managed by focusing on what it would be like to have her on their wedding night, to have her every night afterwards, and whenever he wanted.

'We're sexually in tune, Emma,' he argued, in a desire-thickened voice. 'I can feel it. *You* can feel it. Marry me and I can promise you that that part of our lives will be very fulfilling.'

'You…you think our marriage could really work?'

'I know it could,' he reassured her firmly.

'But we don't love each other.'

'Love is no guarantee of happiness in a relationship, Emma. Surely you can see that. We like each other, and we want each other. We can plan things together with cool heads, instead of hot and sometimes ill-judged hearts. We'll make a great team.'

'You're very persuasive.'

'And you're very lovely.'

She flushed. 'You confuse me.'

'I want you.'

'I'm still not sure why you do.'

'You underestimate yourself.'

'No, I don't think so. I know what I am, and I know I'm not the sort of girl a man like you would normally look at twice. You've asked me to marry you on the rebound, Jason.'

'That's not true. I've asked you to marry me because you're exactly what I want in a wife.'

She frowned at this statement, and in truth it *had* sounded rather cold. Jason regretted it immediately. He leant over and laid a gentle palm against her cheek. 'So what's your answer to be, lovely Emma?' he asked softly. 'Will you marry me or not?'

'You...you were going to wait a month before asking me again,' she replied a little shakily, her eyes searching his as though in fear he was about to kiss her again.

'I've changed my mind. I don't want to waste another moment. Even if you say yes, it will take several weeks to arrange things. The licence alone takes a month, and the banns, three more weeks.'

'Banns?'

'In the church. I'm going to marry you before God, Emma. I'm going to promise to cherish you till death do us part. And you're going to walk down that aisle to me, wearing white, as befits your beautiful innocence.'

'Oh!' she exclaimed, her eyes flooding.

'Don't cry,' he murmured. 'Just say yes, and I'll spend the rest of my life making you happy.'

'You...you promise you'll never be unfaithful?'

'Never!' he vowed heatedly.

'If you are, I'll leave you.'

'If I am, then I'll deserve leaving.'

'So be it. Then, yes, Jason. Yes, I'll marry you.'

CHAPTER FIVE

'WELL?' was the first thing Nancy said to him the following morning. It was his weekend for Saturday morning surgery, unfortunately, otherwise he would have taken Emma engagement-ring-shopping. New-watch-shopping for himself as well.

He contemplated not telling Nancy, but discarded that as futile since he had a fatuous smile plastered all over his face. 'Can you keep a secret, Nancy?' he asked with stupid optimism.

'Dr Steel! What a silly question! Of course I can.'

'She said yes.'

Nancy clapped excitedly. 'Oh, that's wonderful news! Wait till I tell—' She broke off and looked guilty. 'I mean...how long do I have to keep this a secret?' she asked painfully.

'Do you think you might manage till Monday? That's when I'm going to take Emma shopping for a ring.' Whichever doctor took Saturday surgery had Monday off.

'I guess I could,' she said, if a little unhappily. 'But what if Emma tells someone herself beforehand?'

Jason almost laughed. What a terrible disaster that would be. Poor Nancy—to have a scoop and have to sit on it!

He thought about the situation and relented. 'Oh, all right, Nancy. Just let me pop over to the shop and let Emma know I've told you, then you can tell whomever you like.' In truth, he'd already rung Emma once this morning, to make sure she hadn't changed her mind overnight. She hadn't, but had sounded a bit dazed still. She was going to cook him dinner that night, but that was half a day away. A personal visit ASAP would clearly not go astray.

She was just opening the shop when he arrived, her eyes lighting up at the sight of him, before turning a little worried. 'Is there anything wrong?' she asked.

'Not at all. Shall we go inside, or shall I kiss you right out here in the street?'

Her look of shock-horror amused him. 'There's no use thinking you an keep our engagement a secret here in Tindley, Emma,' he said, smiling. 'Nancy already knows. I told her.'

'You *told* her! But why?'

'Because I want everyone to know. Don't you?'

He could see by her face she didn't, and his happy mood immediately deflated. 'What's the problem?' he demanded to know, his ego wounded. 'You're afraid Ratchitt will somehow get to hear you're marrying another man?'

She didn't deny it, and he had difficulty controlling his temper. Taking her elbow, he shepherded her into the privacy of the shop. The last thing he wanted was all of Tindley to overhear their arguing.

'Look, Emma,' he muttered once they were safely alone. 'I thought we had this out the other night. The man's a rotter. And he isn't coming back. When will you get that through your head? Stop being a masochist, for pity's sake, and give yourself a decent chance at happiness.'

Her eyes flashed at him. 'You think I *want* him to come back now?'

'Yes, I do. I think you're fixated on the creep and you won't be happy till you see him again. One part of me wishes he *would* come back, so that you could see just what you've been pining for. My guess is you've romanticised Ratchitt for far too long. If I knew where he was, I'd send him a damned wedding invitation.'

She paled. 'You wouldn't.'

'Too right I would. You think I'm frightened of him? I'd pit myself against the Ratchitts of this world any day, and I know who'd come out on top. Stack us up side by side, Emma, and love or no love, I know who you'd choose in the end!' His voice softened when he saw how stricken she was looking. 'He's low-life, darling. You deserve a lot better than that.'

'You...you called me darling,' she said shakily.

'And so you are,' he crooned, and drew her into his arms. She went willingly, her mouth soft beneath his. He kissed her just long enough and hard enough to make her breathless, and to show her just why she'd agreed to marry him. When he released her, she looked up at him with gratifyingly enslaved eyes. If he felt a tiny stab of guilt for using her blossoming sexuality to his own selfish advantage, then he argued it away in his mind. He was the man for her, wasn't he? He would make her happy, not Dean Ratchitt.

'Now, let's have no more foolish talk,' he said

firmly. 'I'm going to marry the loveliest girl in Tindley and I don't care who knows it!'

The next few weeks were the most amazing in Jason's life. His relationship with Emma deepened considerably with their time spent together. They discovered surprisingly similar tastes in books and movies, both liking character-driven plots you could really get your teeth into. Neither had any patience with mindless violence or horror stories. Science fiction only got the thumbs-up if the characters were believable and didn't have unpronounceable names. Jason had always read a book or watched a video to wind down after a long day's doctoring, and whilst he always bought new books—and only read them once—he liked nothing better than to see a favourite movie several times.

When he'd showed Emma his video collection, she'd expressed delight at spotting some favourites of her own, and insisted they watch every single one together. Over the past month or so they had, and then had such fun listing their top five in order of preference. Jason had been astounded at how close their lists were. They both put *Witness* at number one, and, whilst the next three had been in different order, they'd both selected *Braveheart*, *Chariots of Fire*, and *Tootsie* for numbers two to four. Only in the fifth selection had they differed, Emma liking Jane Austen's *Emma*—which he'd laughingly pronounced a form of nepotism—whilst he'd put in *Blade Runner*.

Yes, Jason was delighted at how the woman he'd chosen with his head and not his heart was working out. Just talking to Emma was great. And with any serious lovemaking sidelined till the wedding, they had a lot of time for just talking.

He discovered that his fiancée, whilst not academically brilliant, was creative, intuitive and sensitive, holding interesting opinions on a wide range of subjects. In the year she'd nursed Ivy, she'd read her aunt the newspaper every day from cover to cover, and had acquired a general knowledge which was surprising. Her memory was excellent. She still read the paper over breakfast every morning, she told him with pride.

Jason also admired her cooking skills, whilst she, in turn, simply admired him. He could feel it, and it fed his confidence where she was concerned. Once their wedding day was on the horizon, he really didn't care if Ratchitt returned.

The trouble was…it wasn't Ratchitt who showed up to spoil things. It was Adele.

It was two weeks before the wedding, a coolish Friday in late October. Doc was taking surgery that afternoon, and Jason was out on house calls. He'd just finished his last call and was heading back to Tindley when his mobile beeped. It was Nancy.

'A call came through for you, Dr Steel,' she said, a bit snippily. 'A lady doctor, no less. She said it was an emergency and she needed to contact you immediately.'

Jason felt his stomach flip over. 'Did she leave her name?'

'Yes. Dr Harvey. She said you would know her numbers off by heart,' Nancy added, suspicion in her tone. 'Anyway, she wants you to ring her back straight away.'

'Right. Thanks, Nancy. Dr Harvey's an old colleague from my Sydney days. Must have a medical problem she needs consulting on,' he found himself babbling. Hell, he could feel Nancy's dark disapproval down the line. The possibility—however remote—of her spreading a rumour around Tindley that Dr Steel was no better than Dean Ratchitt, and had some lady-friend on the side whilst he was courting Emma, brought panic. Emma was so vulnerable in that regard.

'Damn you, Adele,' he growled as he pulled over to the side of the road and dialled the number of the surgery first.

She wasn't there. She was on the road somewhere. Would he like her mobile number?

He said he knew it, which he did. He'd rung the darned thing a million times in his day.

She answered on the third ring.

'Jase?'

He ignored the jolt the sound of her voice made, not to mention the way she shortened his name. She was the only person who'd ever called him that, and he'd liked it straight away. Perhaps she knew the effect it had on him, for she'd always used it a lot, especially in bed. It had been *Yes, Jase; please, Jase,* and *Oh, God, Jase,* all the time, in low, husky whispers. It sent shivers down his spine just thinking about it.

'What do you want, Adele?' he said, quite coldly, determined not to let her see she affected him in any way. But the length of his celibate state didn't help. Only by reminding himself that he was just two weeks from marrying Emma could he keep the image of a nude Adele gyrating on top of him from exploding to the forefront of his mind.

But then she spoke again, and he was in imminent danger of being mentally unfaithful.

'It's great to hear your voice, Jase. I've missed you, darling. Have you missed me?'

Jason cursed her to hell in his mind.

'My secretary said you had an emergency,' he ground out in what he hoped was his best no-I-haven't-missed-you voice.

'It's your brother, Jase. Jerry.'

Jason snapped to attention. He'd sent Jerry the watch and ring, as planned, as well as a wedding invitation, and had received a small thank-you note, but a regret about the wedding. Jerry was chronically shy and didn't like formal dos.

'What about Jerry?'

'He came into the surgery last night with severe abdominal pains. Just by chance, I was the doctor allotted to him. I didn't want to take any chances so I had him admitted to hospital. Thank God I did, because he had a pretty bad night. They've done tests and he has some form of obscure food-poisoning. He's not critical, but he's a very sick man. The specialist said he won't be in the clear for a couple of days. I thought you might want to be with him.'

'What hospital?'

'Royal North Shore.'

'I'll come straight away.' Doc wouldn't mind taking over for the weekend in this situation. Jason had done the same for him when he'd had to go to a funeral in Brisbane a couple of weeks back.

A funeral...

Dear God, he hoped Jerry didn't die. 'How did you find my number, Adele?' he demanded to know.

'Oh, Jase,' she said, and he could hear the smile in her voice, that slow, sexy smile she used to give him as she undulated towards him across the bedroom, peeling off her clothes as she went. 'I've always known where you were. I was just waiting a while till you came to your senses. Six months I was going to give you, remember? It's been more than that now.'

Bulldust, he thought. She hadn't been going to contact him at all, not till this business with Jerry had made it necessary. She just couldn't resist playing *femme fatale*.

'I'll bet you're bored to tears down there in Hicksville,' she went on a droll tone. 'Country towns and country girls just don't have what it takes to keep a city boy happy. And you're a city boy, Jase,' she said, with a low, wicked little laugh. 'Through and through.'

He knew that. It had been a battle to adjust. But he *had* adjusted, and he *liked* his new life. Okay, so it wasn't wildly exciting. There were no first nights at the opera; no dinner parties in penthouses overlooking the harbour; no all-night sex sessions to drive him out of his mind.

But such things were just passing moments of pleasure. They weren't *life*, not the kind of life he wanted.

'Actually, I'm not bored at all,' he countered

coolly. 'I love it here. Fact is, I'm going to be married a fortnight tomorrow.'

She hardly missed a beat. 'No kidding? What happened, Jase? Get some poor little country girl in trouble, did you?'

'Trust you to think something like that. No, Adele, Emma isn't pregnant.'

'Emma. What a sweet goody-two-shoes name! Does she have a sweet goody-two-shoes nature to go with it? Or is she just a little bit naughty sometimes? Does she do for you what I used to do for you, darling? I can't imagine you doing without *that* once in a while.'

'Emma's a nice girl, Adele,' he said icily.

'Nice, is she? Oh, poor Jase. I think you *are* going to be bored. But you can always drop up to Sydney once in a while. Make some excuse to the little wife. A conference is always good for a weekend away.'

'I have no intention of doing any such thing, Adele. I left you seven months ago and you're staying left.'

She laughed. It wasn't a nice laugh. 'You won't forget me that easily, Jase. You might pretend to, but when you're lying in bed with your nice little wife, and having sweet goody-two-shoes sex every night, you'll think of me. I'll guarantee it.'

'I wouldn't count on it, sweetheart,' he snapped back. 'Thank you for doing the right thing by Jerry. It surprises me you didn't just give him an antacid tablet and send him home to die. I guess even the worst doctor in the world gets it right occasionally. Don't call me again, Adele. Goodbye.'

He was shaking by the time he hung up. Literally

shaking. He dropped the phone on the passenger seat and lowered his sweating forehead onto the steering wheel, glowering down at his lap and the evidence of what she'd done to him with just her voice.

Slowly, he pulled himself together, and put his logical mind into gear. Old tapes playing in his head, he decided. Not love. He'd lived with the woman for three years, made love to her countless times, become addicted to her brand of sex. Hard to wipe out any addiction in a few months. She was like a bad habit which was difficult to toss. Yes, his body had responded—out of habit, not out of true feeling. He refused to believe differently.

You won't forget me that easily, Jase…

He groaned, gunned the engine and headed for Tindley.

He didn't tell Emma the woman doctor who'd called was Adele. He wouldn't have told her it was a woman doctor at all except Nancy knew. And what Nancy knew the whole of Tindley would know, eventually. Thank God Adele hadn't given her Christian name!

He lied to Emma a second time as well, saying this particular lady doctor was a colleague from a different surgery from the one he'd worked at. She'd been given his number by Jerry, he said. Women doctors were common amongst GPs, he'd added, when she'd looked worried.

They weren't evil lies, he reasoned. Just little white lies so that Emma would not feel badly or think worrying things while he was away for the weekend.

He might have taken her with him, except he didn't

trust Adele not to show up at the hospital some time. He wasn't fooled by her nonchalant attitude over the phone. Adele hadn't taken at all well to the 'woman scorned' label. After his verbal insults today, he had no doubt she would love the opportunity to put a spanner in the works of *his* happiness. He didn't think she'd go out of her way to do that—such as a trip to Tindley—but his coming to Sydney was an opportunity she might seize. Someone as soft and sensitive as Emma would be a perfect victim for her brand of malice. Adele would leave no stone unturned to cut away at any confidence Emma had in their marriage working.

No, Emma and Adele had to be kept apart.

Fortunately, Emma was up to her eyes making her wedding dress, and was planning on finishing it that weekend. Jason was glad he didn't have to argue against her coming with him, as that might have made her suspicious. She didn't seem to mind his going, either. She could be a very independent little thing, happy with her own company.

Jason liked her independence. And her lack of material greed. He'd offered to buy her a dress if she couldn't afford one, but she'd refused. She'd given him a warm look at the time and said no, she *wanted* to make her dress. She was a good seamstress, she'd said, and he didn't doubt it. Her tapestries and collages were incredible, and snapped up by buyers the moment they were displayed on the sweet shop walls.

Not that she made much money out of them. The materials and framing ate into her profit. But it was a satisfying hobby and one which had brought in some good pocket money over the years, she'd explained when he'd wanted to discuss her financial situation. Not that he wanted any of her money, he'd quickly added. Whatever she earned was hers to do with as she pleased. Plus anything she inherited from Ivy. He wanted none of it.

She'd listened carefully, then told him Ivy hadn't owned much except the house and shop. He'd been dead right about the shop not bringing in much income as well. Less than twenty thousand a year. Still, Emma said she wanted to keep on working in the shop after their marriage, at least till she had a baby to care for, after which she'd find someone to run it. She didn't want to sell, or even rent out the rest of house. She was going to turn those rooms into a craft club, where the local women could come and work and chat and have a good time.

Jason thought that was a great idea, and said so. He supposed she wouldn't have got much for the rent, and what was money, anyway? It didn't make you happy. He was seeing that more and more these days.

Of course, it wasn't good to be poor, either.

But enough was enough.

'When will you be back?' Emma asked him as she watched him pack. She was sitting on the bed which would eventually be their marriage bed, a huge high brass number which had the comfiest of mattresses and didn't squeak, thankfully.

He looked at her sitting there, swinging her dainty feet, and felt an overwhelming surge of desire. What would she do, he wondered, if he started making love to her, not gently, but fiercely? If he pushed her back on the bed and mercilessly took her past the point of no return?

He could do it. He knew he could.

He'd felt the rising sexual tension in her over the weeks of waiting, weeks when he'd kissed her and held her, cuddled and caressed her till they were both breathing heavily and both wanting more. Last night, however, she'd totally lost it, which had been good for his ego but bad for his own level of frustration. She'd actually begged him not to stop, and it had taken one heck of an effort to deny her, with his hand sliding up under her dress at the time.

But he had, telling her highly agitated self that he knew she'd hate him afterwards if he went on. They only had to last two more weeks. What was two weeks when compared to a lifetime?

She'd shaken her head at him, her face flushed, her whole body still trembling. 'I wish I'd never started this nonsense.'

'It's not nonsense, Emma. It's sweet, and it's special, as you are special. I can't say I was thrilled by the idea in the beginning. But now I wouldn't have it any other way.'

She'd looked up at him with something close to love in her eyes, and he'd been blown away. He thought of that look now and abandoned all plans of a forced seduction. She would not look at him like that afterwards. He was sure of that as well.

'I can't say when I'll be back,' he told her truthfully. 'It'll depend on Jerry's condition. But I'll keep you posted. I have to be back to do morning surgery on Monday. At the very latest I could drive back very early Monday morning. At least the traffic wouldn't be so bad then.' With the advent of warmer weather, the tourist season was on the move again, and the Princes Highway was always busy.

'I'll miss you,' she said softly. He glanced over his shoulder at her and their eyes locked. Hers were like large, shimmering green pools, and he felt himself dissolving. Her mouth looked soft and inviting, as did her whole body, clothed as usual in one of her softly flowing feminine dresses. It was a simple and sweet style, with tiny mauve flowers all over it.

He wanted to rip it to shreds.

'I'll miss you too,' he returned, but stayed with his packing. Hell, if he kissed her now…

She fell silent, and he glanced over his shoulder a second time. Her hands were in her lap and she was twisting her engagement ring around and around. The diamond sparkled in the sunshine which was coming in the window and slanting across the bed. It wasn't a huge diamond, but it was what she'd chosen. Four smaller emeralds flanked the shoulders, the same green as her lovely eyes. He planned on giving her a matching eternity ring on their wedding night. The jeweller had secretly made it up for him after she'd chosen her engagement ring and he was to collect it next week.

'Is there something wrong, Emma?' he asked.

She looked up and smiled a taut little smile. 'No, I suppose not. I'm being silly. It's just that I had this feeling. You know…like someone was walking over my grave? A premonition. You…you will be careful, won't you, Jason? I mean, driving around those busy Sydney roads.'

He came over and sat down beside her, taking her by the shoulders and looking deep into her eyes. 'I'll be very careful,' he promised. 'Nothing, and I mean nothing, is going to stop me coming back to you.'

'You promise?'

'You have my solemn oath.'

Her sigh was deep. 'That's all right, then.'

Without kissing her, he rose and returned to his packing.

The trip up was a nightmare. Too many cars and trucks, and too many hold-ups. The road being dug up in too many places.

And then it started to rain.

It was well after dark by the time he turned his car into the hospital car park, later by the time he found Jerry's ward. His new watch said ten to nine as he strode up to the ward work station where he introduced himself as a doctor as well as Jerry's brother, thereby stopping any officious nonsense about it being after visiting hours. Then he asked if he could speak to the specialist in charge of Jerry's case.

The sister, who was an attractive woman in her thirties, smiled at him and said that unfortunately he wouldn't be able to speak to that particular doctor till morning. But Jerry's GP was somewhere in the building. Also unfortunately, they'd given his brother a sedative not long before, and he was probably asleep. But he was welcome to sit by his brother for as long as he liked. He was in 4F, last room down on the left.

Jason walked down the highly polished corridor to 4F, a long thin room which had six beds, though only four were filled. Jerry was lying in the furthest bed from the door. He had a window with a view over the city, but Jerry wasn't seeing any view at the moment. He *was* sound asleep.

Adele, Jason saw with some relief, was nowhere in sight. But he had no doubt she would show up soon. The thought rattled him somewhat.

He found thankful distraction in his brother's condition, inspecting Jerry's pupils and taking his pulse. When he read the chart at the foot of the bed, Jason felt momentarily nauseous at how touch and go it had been. Jerry's blood pressure had been appallingly low at one time, his temperature sky-high. He'd had seizures during the night as well.

No doubt he should have been in an intensive care unit, but he was a non-paying public patient, so what could you expect? Not presidential treatment, that was for sure. Still, things seemed to have stabilised, and he would probably pull through. He looked like hell, though.

Jason put the chart back and walked over to the window. He stared down at the city lights. Pretty spectacular-looking. Certainly not the unsophisticated colonial outpost the rest of world occasionally imagined. Sydney throbbed during the day, and hummed at night. It was an exciting and beautiful city, full of exciting and beautiful people.

'Hello, Jase... I've been waiting for you...'

Her husky voice curled around his gut and pulled him slowly round.

The sight of her, however, had a surprisingly different effect.

She was standing there at the foot of Jerry's bed, wearing one of those sexy little black numbers which had always turned him on. Not a suit, this time, but a dress, a short, chic crêpe sheath which looked as if it had been sewn on, it was so tight. The blatant outline of erect nipples shouted she wasn't wearing a bra, which wasn't a surprise. When did Adele ever wear a bra?

The shortness of the skirt suggested she'd opted against suspenders in favour of sheer shiny black pantyhose, the expensive kind which never ran, no matter how many times they were man-handled. Her feet were shod in the sort of sexy strappy high heels guaranteed to raise most men's blood pressure.

Jason's heart didn't miss a beat.

She sashayed a little closer, perhaps to show him she could walk in them quite well.

Practice did give one a wide range of professional skills, he thought cynically, as his eyes raked over her.

She took his thorough appraisal for interest, fairly preening before him. What she didn't know was the reality of her had had the opposite effect of her voice over the phone. That had stirred old memories, those old tapes in his head. Powerful old tapes. Adele in the flesh stirred nothing in him but a rueful surprise that he'd ever found her attractive, let alone addictive.

After being with someone as genuinely lovely as Emma—inside and out—Adele looked the hard piece she basically was. Her short dyed black hair was too harsh around her too pale make-up. She was wearing too much black around her eyes, too dark a lipstick on her full mouth and too much perfume all over her body. It fairly swamped him in its overpoweringly musky scent.

Sure, she still had a striking figure, with legs up to her armpits, but even that was now too much. He preferred Emma's tiny daintiness. He preferred Emma's lack of artifice. He preferred everything about Emma.

The worry that he might still be harbouring a lasting passion for Adele disappeared like a magician's assistant, and the relief was overwhelming. He was free of her at last. Free to forge a future with Emma without any hangovers from the past. His elation produced a real high.

He looked up at Adele's sultry face and laughed.

She pouted angrily. 'Why are you laughing at me like that?'

'I wasn't laughing at you, Adele. I was laughing at myself.'

'Meaning?'

'Meaning I've been a fool. Look, I don't hold any malice towards you, Adele, but you're wasting your time here. Go and find yourself another poor ignorant idiot you can infatuate with your undoubtedly skilful technique. I don't want it—or you—any more.'

Disbelief soon gave way to a dark determination. 'Give me five minutes and I'll bet I could change your mind about that.'

'Five minutes? Here and now?'

'Right here and right now,' she mouthed provocatively. 'Jerry's unconscious. We could pull the curtain around his bed.' She began to do just that, the action bringing her closer.

He snatched the curtain out of her hands and threw it back, eyeing her with a savage look which rooted her to the spot. 'Now listen to me, you miserable excuse for a human being and a doctor,' he hissed. 'I wouldn't let you touch me if you were the last woman on earth and the existence of the human race depended on it. You make my skin crawl, do you know that? Which is what you should be doing. Crawling, like the low-life serpent you are. Go crawl on back into your hole, darling, and give us decent folk some fresh air to breathe.'

She didn't say a word, just stared at him, her cold black eyes filling with hate.

He knew he'd gone too far. Far too far. But it was too late now.

Still without saying a word, she spun round on those dangerously high stilettos, and, without teetering a millimetre, stalked from the room.

Jason was left to watch her go, and to worry about what form her vengeance might take.

CHAPTER SIX

IT WAS a worrisome weekend, despite Jerry making a good recovery on the Saturday, and despite several phone calls to Emma eliciting a happy brightness from her which Jason doubted could be faked. The dreaded Adele had clearly not zapped down to Tindley during his absence to stir up trouble.

Each phone call home should have brought relief. Instead, it created more tension in him, an irrational fear that everything he'd been working towards and looking forward to was about to be destroyed. His relationship with Emma. Their marriage. His future.

He set off for the five-hour drive back to Tindley mid-afternoon on Sunday, leaving behind a much improved Jerry, but taking with him an escalating tension. He had to stop himself from speeding, only his promise to Emma to drive carefully holding him back.

But he wanted to see her for himself and make sure everything was all right. He drove into Tindley shortly after seven, parked outside the sweet shop and went straight round to her back door, knocking impatiently.

The moment she opened it, he knew he was too late. For as long as he lived Jason would always remember her expression at that moment. Never had he seen such dismay and despair. Her face was dead white, her eyes red-rimmed. That she'd been crying for hours was obvious.

He reacted as any man would. With a helpless, hopeless fury.

'What, in God's name, did that vicious, vindictive cow say to you?'

Her chin came up, as it did sometimes, and she eyed him suddenly with a chilling dislike. 'I presume you're speaking about Adele. Dr Adele Harvey, to give her her full name. The woman you lived with for three years. The woman who rang you about your brother on Friday. The same woman you made love to for hours on end this weekend.'

'No!' he burst out, and, launching himself into the house, he grabbed her upper arms and kicked the door shut behind him. 'No, no, no!' he repeated loudly, shaking her. 'A thousand times no!'

She glared down at the brutal grip on her arms till he released her.

'Which part is wrong, Jason?' she asked coldly. 'Which one of the many lies you told me isn't a lie?'

He grimaced at how bad things must look to her. 'Look, I only lied about who rang me because I was afraid you'd think the wrong things. And I was right, by the look of things. You did. You *do*! Damn it, Emma, I didn't sleep with Adele. I saw her briefly at the hospital on Friday night, and, yes, she did make a pass at me, but, no, I didn't touch her. And, no, I'm not still in love with her. In fact, I said some pretty nasty things, and I knew afterwards that she'd get even. And she has. She's rung you up and fed you a whole truckful of lies.'

Emma said nothing, just looked at him and started shaking her head.

'I did not sleep with her!' he shouted.

'I don't believe you. By the way, she didn't ring, Jason. She came in person. She was here, this afternoon, in this very kitchen.'

'Oh, God,' Jason groaned.

'Seeing her was worth a thousand words. She's everything I could never be. Strikingly beautiful. Incredibly smart. Stunningly sophisticated. No man would choose me over her if he had a real choice.'

Jason was appalled. Adele must have really put on a show. Toned down the make-up. Dressed more sedately. Acted as though she had feelings.

'You *had* to get out of Sydney, didn't you?' Emma threw at him, and he gaped. 'It was your patient who died. It was you who was shamefully neglectful, not Adele. She told me all about it.'

Jason's mouth finally snapped shut. 'Really?' he grated out. 'Do go on. I'm fascinated to hear the rest of the script of the best performance since Scarlett O'Hara in *Gone With The Wind*.'

'You can scoff all you like, but I know the truth when I hear it. She was crying,' Emma flung at him with a wealth of emotion. 'Crying her heart out. She told me she'd never loved any man as much as she'd loved you. But after what happened with the little boy she just couldn't work with you any more, or be with you any more. She finally told you to leave, and you did, without a backward glance.'

Jason could hardly believe his ears! He might have laughed if he hadn't been seeing his life go down the tubes at a frightening rate.

'She knew then that you'd never loved her at all,

that all you'd ever wanted was success and sex. She said your greed and ambition knew no bounds. You were eaten up with the idea of money because you'd once been so poor. She said she thought she had no feeling left for you, but when she saw you on Friday night, and you looked so upset about your brother, she felt sorry for you. And, of course, you *are* a very handsome man, Jason. No one could deny that.'

Well, thank heaven for small mercies, he thought bitterly.

'She asked you back to her place, just to give you a place to sleep for the night, but when you started making love to her she just couldn't resist. She said you always were a wonderful lover. Very...skilled. The next morning she wanted to tell you to go, and not come back that night, but she didn't have the strength of will. She hadn't had a lover since you left, and she's been so lonely.'

Jason was shaking his head in disbelief, but Emma just ignored him, determined, it seemed, to relay every lie Adele had fed her.

'By this morning she felt bitterly ashamed, even more so when you told her you were going to be married, to a simple country girl who would look after you like a king but never question what you did or where you went. She said you told her sex with me would bore you to death, but you aimed to supplement your bland day-to-day diet with more exotic fare from time to time. Women you'd met over on the coast. A widow or two you'd met during your rounds. The occasional trip to Sydney—and her.'

'Oh, *please*,' he groaned, but Emma swept on, regardless.

'She said after you left for the hospital this morning she kept thinking about me, a fellow woman, about to be used and deceived so cruelly. She drove down to apologise for what she'd done and to warn me to break off my engagement to you. And that's exactly what I'm going to do.' Her eyes filled and she began to take off her ring.

'You stop that right there!' Jason raged.

And she did, wide, tear-filled eyes flying to his.

'She lied to you, Emma. Can't you see that? Hell, I can prove that boy wasn't my patient. There are records. Documents. Death certificates. Besides, don't you think Doc Brandewilde had me checked out before he took me on as a partner? My reputation as a doctor is second to none. I can also prove where I stayed on Friday and Saturday night. In a hotel in North Sydney. Nowhere near Adele's place at Palm Beach. The man at the desk would remember me. I had breakfast in the public dining room both mornings. If you like I'll take you up there personally, so that you can ask around.'

Jason saw he was beginning to get through to her. Her mouth was dropping open and a big dollop of doubt was muddying that shimmering but clear green gaze.

'Then there's my calls to you,' he argued with ruthless logic. 'All made either from the hospital or the hotel. Phone records would prove that. None were made from Adele's number. You know how often I rang you. If I was supposed to be in bed with Adele half the weekend I would have had to call you some of the time from her place, wouldn't I? Think, Emma. Don't let her do this to us. Don't let her spoil what we have, which is something very special. Very precious. That's what's killing her. That I don't love her any more and that I've found happiness with someone else. She doesn't really want me, but she doesn't want you to have me, either. I promised you I would never be unfaithful to you and I haven't.'

'But how...how can I be sure of that?' she cried plaintively. 'There's no proof. If it were me who'd been unfaithful to you, at least there'd be proof!'

'You shouldn't need proof, Emma, not if you know me at all. You have my word.'

'Your word...'

'Yes,' he said. 'Or isn't that good enough?'

When she didn't say anything, his shoulders sagged, all his energy suddenly draining out of him.

'That's it, then,' he said wearily. 'We have no future anyway, if you don't trust me.'

When he went to walk away she grabbed his shoulder. 'If what you say is true...then that woman is truly wicked.'

'She is, Emma. Believe me.'

'Then how could you ever have loved her?'

'I thought you said someone being wicked was no barrier to love?'

'No, I meant *doing* something wicked. Not *being* wicked. Truly wicked.'

'Ahh... So your beloved Dean isn't truly wicked? He just made one mistake. That's a joke, Emma, and you know it. He'd been sleeping around in this town for years before he turned his attentions to you. And he didn't confine himself to single women, either, from what I've heard. Nothing's sacred with him, provided he gets his end in!'

'Don't be disgusting!'

'You have to be disgusting when you're talking about men like him, and women like Adele. They're both tarred with the same brush. They're selfish and amoral and mean. What they want, and can't have, they try to destroy.'

Her face began to crumple. 'I…I suppose you're right…'

He stepped forward and folded her into his arms before she could burst into tears, holding her close and stroking her hair. 'We can't let them spoil things for us, Emma. We have to stay strong. And stick together.'

He felt her lungs fill on a deep breath, then empty in a series of small, quivering shudders. 'It's so hard,' she said.

'Life *is* hard, Emma. But people sometimes make it harder by picking the wrong partners. Dean was as bad for you as Adele was for me.'

She drew back and looked up at him with glistening green eyes. 'Did…did you still find her attractive, Jason?'

'No. Not one little bit.'

'I find that hard to believe. She's very striking-looking. And so tall and stylish.'

'I much prefer you, Emma.'

'Do you still want to wait till our wedding night?'

'Yes.'

Perversely, she looked put out.

'Do *you*?' he asked gently.

'Yes. No. Oh, I don't know.' She pulled out of his arms and began to pace agitatedly around the kitchen. 'I don't know anything any more. All I know is that I can't stop thinking about it.'

'It?'

She ground to a halt on the opposite side of the table and threw him a reproachful look. 'You know very well what I'm talking about, Jason. Don't be cruel. It's all very well for you. You've been there, done that. You don't know what it's like to lie there in bed at night and wonder and worry.'

'What do you wonder and worry about?'

'Everything!'

Jason wasn't about to tell her he was a bit worried himself. He wanted to make their wedding night wonderful for her, but her virginity might prove a problem. From what he'd gleaned, a first-time experience could be pretty painful. Yet he wanted to give her nothing but pleasure. She deserved it. He would have to use every bit of knowledge and skill he had to ensure that she would experience *some* pleasure at least.

But first he had to allay her fears. Fear caused tension, and tension often caused more pain.

'It's going to be fine, Emma,' he said softly. 'You're a very responsive girl. Worrying isn't going to help things. Making the sex good is *my* job. Leave it up to me.'

Emma stared at him. 'She...she said you were a wonderful lover...'

'How nice of her,' came his frosty reply. 'Are you worried she was lying about that as well?'

'No. I'm worried you're going to find me a very big disappointment.'

'I doubt that, Emma.' Hell, he'd been aching to make her his own for weeks now. He'd enjoy himself, no matter what! 'Just don't expect too much too soon. Really good sex can sometimes take a little time.'

She frowned.

'And talking about it is the kiss of death,' he added with a wry smile. 'So shall we stop, and curl up together on the sofa and watch the Sunday movie? It's going on eight-thirty.'

She looked at him as though he was insane. 'No, no, I don't think so, Jason. I've had a pretty upsetting day, and my mind is too full to watch a movie.'

'Oh. Oh, all right.' He could never get used to the way women liked to wallow in their feelings. Now that she knew Adele had been lying, she should be happy. *He* was. 'I'll drop in for breakfast, shall I?'

'If you like.'

He frowned at her coolness. 'You're not still angry with me, are you, Emma?'

'You *did* lie to me, Jason.'

'But with the best of intentions, darling.'

His using that term of endearment did not go down well at all. 'Don't try to soft soap me, Jason. You lied. You didn't trust *me* to trust *you*. I hope you won't make a habit of that.'

He blinked at her stern tone, and the uncompromising glint in her eyes. She was a lot tougher than he'd realised. And quite stubborn about some things.

But so was he. 'I repeat, Emma. I did what I did because I didn't want you to worry. People tell little white lies sometimes.'

'I understand that. But I won't be taken for a fool. Or some simple country girl who won't ask questions.'

Jason sighed. It seemed Adele's malicious lies could not be wiped away so easily. He would have to win Emma's trust back with actions, rather than words. He vowed never to go anywhere without her for a long, long time. Not that he should have to. Soon, they would be married, and then they would spend every spare moment together.

His loins leapt at the thought. He could hardly wait!

CHAPTER SEVEN

'JASON, do stop fidgeting!' Martha hissed from the front pew. 'It took me ages to arrange that tie for you and it's perfect. Leave it alone.'

Jason lowered his hands, which were shaking slightly.

This marriage business wasn't as easy as he'd thought it would be. Certainly not this part, with him standing alone at the foot of the altar and a whole churchful of people staring expectantly, first up at him, then down the still empty aisle.

No best man stood by his side to calm him. He didn't have one, hadn't thought he needed one. Emma had decided against bridesmaids. She didn't have any girlfriends her age, she'd explained, her intensive nursing of Ivy preventing her from socialising this past year or so. She didn't have any close relatives, either. No one she could ask to walk her down the aisle and give her away.

Doc had agreed to do the honours, and he and his wife, Martha, were going to sign the certificate as witnesses. They weren't having a formal reception, either. Officially it was a quiet little wedding, but they'd issued a general invitation to everyone in town to come to the church, where Jason had organised for drinks and sandwiches to be served outside afterwards, weather permitting. Then, after photos were taken, the wedding cake would be duly cut and small speeches made under the large oak tree near the church steps.

Once tradition was satisfied, Jason was going to whisk Emma straight off on their honeymoon, an unknown destination on the coast where they would spend a week before they had to be back. Jason hadn't felt he could take any more time off than a week after only being at the practice for so short a time.

A quick glance at his new watch showed him it was twenty-five past three, yet the wedding had been booked for three.

Where in heaven's name *was* she? It wasn't as though she had to go far. The church was right in town, less than a minute's drive from the sweet shop. You could walk the distance if you had to!

Linking his hands agitatedly behind his back, he moved from foot to foot, and waited. The minutes dragged on. It had to be three thirty by now, and still…no sight of her.

She's changed her mind, he thought. She isn't coming.

Jason closed his eyes as the ghastly possibility took shape in his mind. She'd been different since the disaster with Adele. Quieter and more distant. She hadn't wanted to watch movies with him, hadn't wanted him to touch her or kiss her. Sometimes he'd caught her looking at him with watchful eyes, as though she didn't know what he was any more.

He'd done his best to reassure her. But the bottom line was their relationship had been damaged by what he'd done. He should have been honest with her. He could see that now. He was going to pay for his mistake, and pay dearly. She wasn't going to marry him.

'She's here,' Martha whispered to him, and Jason's eyes flew open in time to see that the minister was in place in front of the altar and everyone else's heads had swivelled round to face the back.

He felt sick with relief.

The organ started up with the 'Bridal March' and there she was…his bride…his Emma, floating down the aisle towards him in the most gloriously feminine wedding dress he'd ever seen, a fantastic concoction of chiffon and lace which fitted tightly around her bust before flowing right down to the ground in soft folds. The neckline was dangerously low-cut, displaying more of her breasts than he'd ever seen—or even felt—before. Tight lace sleeves encased her arms, in which she carried an elegant sheaf of white lilies. The soft folds of the skirt swirled around her legs as she walked, clinging to her slender thighs in the most tantalising fashion. A pearl choker adorned her elegant neck. A short lace veil covered most of her pretty face. A long, lace-edged net veil trailed out behind her, completing the truly stunning image.

That she had made her dress and veil awed him. That she would make such a sexy style surprised and aroused him.

He would have liked to see her eyes as she approached, but they were hidden from him by the veil. Only her mouth was visible.

It was totally unmade-up, he noted with some surprise. She usually wore lipstick, if only a pale colour. Had she forgotten to put it on? He could appreciate that nerves could make one forget anything. *He'd* had to go back for their rings. And arranging a simple tie had been beyond him.

He smiled a little nervously at her, but she didn't smile back. Neither did Doc.

Jason's stomach dropped to the floor. Something was wrong. He wasn't sure what, but something...

He frowned at Doc, but he was already turning away to join Martha in the front pew. When Jason took Emma's hand, it was trembling uncontrollably.

He wanted to ask her what was wrong, but the minister had already started the simple and traditional ceremony they'd chosen. Soon, Doc was coming forward to say his bit, and they were both vowing, 'I do.' Jason tried to sound cool and confident, but Emma's voice was small and strained.

The exchange of wedding bands was similarly tense, with Emma's hands shaking so badly he had to help her slide the ring on him.

Nothing, however, had been as fraught with danger as the part where the minister had asked if there was anyone here who knew of any reason why these two should not be declared man and wife. Jason had been holding Emma's hand at the time, and felt her fingers flinch, then freeze, felt her holding herself so stiffly that he worried she was on the verge of a faint.

And then it came to him. Why she was late. Why she was still in such a state.

She'd been waiting one last time, hoping that Ratchitt would return at the last moment to save her from marrying a man she didn't love.

Jason's emotions began to churn as he watched her

stiffly held form. What was she thinking or silently hoping for at this moment? That her long-lost love would suddenly stand up there in the organ loft, screaming at her not to do it? And if he did, what would *she* do? Pick up the skirt of her wedding dress and run away from him into her lover's arms, drive off into the sunset in the old rust-bucket of a utility he was sure to drive?

Perhaps. Jason didn't know. And he could hardly ask. All he could do was hold his breath, as she was holding hers, and wait till the ghastly moment passed.

It did, and he could almost feel the huge sigh of relief which rippled through the congregation.

Damn it, what did they know that he didn't?

They knew Ratchitt; that was what. Knew how crazy Emma had been about him. Knew the sort of man he was. Jason accepted that if and when he *did* turn up it would not be a good day.

But he refused to worry about that today. Today was his wedding day. Today, Emma was marrying *him*.

'I now pronounce you Man and Wife!' the minister said loudly, and the congregation burst into spontaneous applause.

Jason was stunned. His head turned to see a sea of smiling faces. They were genuinely happy, he realised. Happy for him and his bride. Happy for the little local girl with the broken heart who'd finally found a decent man to stand by her side. He felt humbled again, as he had several times since coming to Tindley. He hoped he would never let his lovely bride

or this town down. He sure as heck aimed to give
both his best shot.

He suddenly realised the minister had said he might
kiss the bride.

Filled with resolve to be everything she could want
in a husband, he turned to her with a warmly confident
smile on his face and lifted the lace veil. Her eyes
speared him with doubt. For they were shimmering
with tears and clinging to his with a pleading desperation he could not understand.

What was it she wanted him to do?

'Emma?' he whispered on a puzzled, pained note.

'Just kiss me, Jason. Kiss me...'

So he did. Gently. Sweetly.

But it seemed that wasn't what she wanted at all,
for she reached up and cupped his face with determined hands, digging her fingertips into his cheeks
and drawing his mouth more firmly down upon hers.
Parting her lips, she sent her tongue forward as she
had never done before, entwining it around his in an
erotic dance.

It blew him away, and before he knew it it was *her*
face imprisoned within *his* hands, and he was kissing
her as a lover might before sweeping his woman under him in bed, his tongue surging deep into her
mouth.

By the time he released her, his ears were ringing
and hot blood was thrumming through his veins. He
stared with wide eyes down at her, expecting he knew
not what.

She stared back up at him, her glazed gaze gradually clearing to an expression of the most heart-felt

relief and heartbreaking gratitude. Jason almost reeled under its impact, and its implication. She was grateful to him. *Grateful!*

Hell on earth, he agonised with a flash of stark realisation. He didn't want her gratitude. He wanted her *love*!

Jason almost laughed. He'd thought he'd worked it all out. He'd thought he'd got round the problem of falling madly in love with a woman. The insanity of it all. The blindness. The uncontrollable passion. And the ultimate pain.

Yet he'd done it again. Not only done it again, but done it much more dangerously than ever before, because he not only loved this woman, he liked and respected her, wanted and admired her.

He would *never* fall out of love with Emma.

Yet she would *never* fall in love with *him*.

She'd told him. Quite emphatically.

Of course, underneath, he hadn't really believed her. He saw that now. His ego had fooled him, letting him think he could win her heart in the end. But after today's performance he doubted that would happen. Ratchitt had her heart. He would always have her heart...

The hurt was unbearable. He could not stand it. *He* wanted her heart. He wanted all of her. Oh, God!

You can't have everything in life, son...

'Jason?'

He blinked, his eyes clearing to see she was now looking up at him with worried eyes.

Gathering himself, he found a smile from somewhere. 'It's all right,' he said softly, and patted her hand. 'I just need something to eat.'

'We have to sign the register first.'

'Yes, of course.'

'And the photographer wants some extra shots in the church.'

'Ahh...'

Somehow he made it through everything. The signing. The photos. The cake-cutting and the speeches. At last he was helping Emma into the car and climbing in behind the wheel. Doc obligingly removed the tin cans which some boys had tied to the bumper bar. Jason told him to leave the 'JUST MARRIED' sign stuck on the back window. That could easily be removed once they were out on the road.

His mood brightened once they were on their way, the despair which had been hovering lifting. Logic came to his rescue once more. He'd overreacted back there in the church. Seen things with an overly black pessimism.

So he loved her. That wasn't bad. That wasn't wrong. She was his wife, after all.

Okay, so he couldn't tell her he did. Not yet, anyway. She wouldn't believe him at this stage. She'd warned him never to tell her he loved her when he didn't.

But he could *show* her he loved her. By his actions. By being whatever she wanted him to be.

His mind flew back to the way she'd kissed him in the church, and the penny dropped. She didn't want *too* much tenderness in his lovemaking. She wanted passion. She wanted to be swept off her feet. She didn't want to think, or to remember...

Jason gritted his teeth as the spectre of Ratchitt loomed once again in his mind. In a way, it would have been better if he *had* showed up some time. Jason could fight a real live man, but not a romantic memory. Ratchitt was like an evil spirit hovering over their life together, a third party trying to climb with malicious intent into their marriage bed.

Well, there would be no third party tonight, he vowed. Emma would know who was in bed with her, know who was her first lover, if not her first love.

Jason Steel. That was who. Her husband, and the man who *really* loved her.

CHAPTER EIGHT

'YOU were fairly late arriving at the church,' he said, lightly, and not at all accusingly.

They were barely ten minutes into the drive and she hadn't said a word. Jason had just climbed back into the car after ripping off the 'JUST MARRIED' sign. Emma had spent the short stop taking off her veil and laying it carefully on the back seat. Now she was back, facing the front, pulling at the pins which had anchored her hair up on top of her head. It tumbled down around her ears and neck in a mass of silky blonde waves.

Jason believed she'd heard him, but was pretending not to.

'Last-minute nerves?' he suggested, his hand reaching for the key but not turning it yet.

Her sidewards frown seemed innocent enough, but her hands were twisted tightly in her lap. Far too tightly.

'The reason you were late,' he repeated calmly, even while his own stomach clenched down hard.

'Oh. Yes. Nerves.' And she looked away from him through the passenger window.

Jason decided the only way to defuse the power this man had over Emma—and himself—was to bring him out in the open. 'Emma,' he said gently, his hand lifting from the ignition, 'let's not keep secrets from each other.'

Her head whipped round, her face flushing with guilt. 'What do you mean? Secrets?'

'Look, I know you were thinking about Ratchitt this afternoon in the church. I dare say he's the reason you were late, because you had some last-minute doubts. It's perfectly understandable and I'm not upset at all.'

What a pathetic liar he was! It had turned him inside out. Even Emma gave him a look which suggested his lack of anger was incredible.

But to tell her the truth—that he'd been beside himself with the blackest of jealousies—would not help him achieve his goal of taking away the mystery and the magic of this man whom Emma thought she still loved.

'I won't be angry with you,' he said, all the while mentally gnashing his teeth. 'I promise. So you can admit it. You *were* thinking about him, weren't you?'

'Yes,' she confessed in a strangled voice.

Jason swallowed. 'Tell me about him.'

Her eyes widened, then jerked away. 'No,' she said agitatedly. 'No, I don't want to. You can't make me.'

Jason had never felt so angry. Or so impotent.

Slowly, she turned back to face him, her expression quite determined. 'I've made my choice, Jason,' she told him. 'And it's you. Believe me when I tell you that if Dean had come to me today, before the wedding, and begged me not to marry you, but to marry him instead, then my answer would have been no. I would still be sitting here with you. So please…don't spoil our honeymoon by bringing Dean up again.'

Jason wasn't sure whether to be pleased or not. If only she hadn't sounded so bitter. If only her voice had been warm and passionate, and not so chillingly valiant, as though such a decision would have entailed an awful sacrifice on her part.

'I don't know what to say,' he said, truthfully enough.

She stared at him for a few seconds, then smiled a strange little smile. 'You could tell me you like my dress. You haven't mentioned it yet. Not once.'

And he hadn't. He'd been so rattled by what had happened in the church that he'd hardly been able to think straight afterwards, let alone remember his manners. Her gentle reproof reminded him how much such compliments mattered to women at the best of times. That he'd forgotten to voice his delight in her wedding dress was unforgiveable.

Saying sorry was highly inadequate, so he let his eyes speak volumes as they roved hotly over her, lingering on the provocative curves of her tantalisingly exposed breasts. How her nipples hadn't popped out was a downright miracle. He gulped down the lump in his throat, his follow-up words thickened with a maddeningly uncomfortable desire.

'When I saw you coming down the aisle in that dress, I thought I'd died and gone to heaven. Never has a bride looked so radiantly beautiful. Or so damned sexy,' he added drily. 'And then, when you kissed me like that…' He shook his head. 'You've never kissed me like that before, Emma.' She'd accepted his tongue in the past, but never used hers. Just thinking about the way it had snaked around his was turning him on again.

'Yes, I know,' she said, her eyes never leaving his. 'But you're my husband now. And I'm your wife. There's no reason for either of us to hold back any more, is there?'

'Hell,' he said. 'Don't say things like that, or I'll make love to you here and now.'

'If…if you like…'

He blinked at her. She could not possibly want him to make love to her here, in the car, in broad daylight. The thought that she'd been brought up to believe marriage entailed a female sacrificing herself on the altar of forcible conjugal relations repulsed him. His face must have revealed his thoughts because she looked distressed.

'Don't you want to make love to me, Jason?'

'Yes, of course I do. But I know women. They like making love in more comfortable conditions than this. You said the other week you were worried about what our wedding night would be like for you. Trust me when I tell you it's better we wait till later, when we have total privacy.' A car zoomed by at that moment, then another, highlighting the unsuitability of this setting for any form of real intimacy.

'Yes, I guess you're right…'

Now she looked disappointed. He didn't know what to do for the best.

'Emma, trust me.'

'I do, Jason.'

'Good. Then we wait a little longer.' Even if it killed him.

Against his better judgement, he leant over and kissed her, just to take that hurt look off her face. Her mouth was soft and melting under his, and his heart turned over and over. He could not help it. He pried her lips open again and waited to see if she would do it again.

She did, even more sensually than before, her tongue an erotically lethal weapon as it explored his whole mouth. Hell on earth, he thought, and abruptly lifted his head.

Her lips remained provocatively open for a few seconds, her mouth wet and inviting, her eyes tightly shut. Her sigh, when it came, was long and shuddering.

He turned from her to start the car, but not before he vowed to make her shudder again tonight, often, and with satisfaction, not frustration.

The unit he'd booked for their honeymoon was in Narooma, a small seaside town south-east of Tindley and only an hour's drive away. Narooma was quite a popular tourist spot during the summer holidays, being exactly halfway between Sydney and Melbourne, with a kind climate and lots to do. Fishing. Swimming. Boating. Bushwalking.

Restaurants were plentiful, as were clubs which provided plenty of entertainment.

And then there was the golf course, for which Narooma was quite famous. It was listed amongst the top ten courses in Australia, with several holes overlooking the Pacific Ocean, and one providing a chasm to drive over from tee to the green. Jason enjoyed a game of golf occasionally, and Emma had agreed to caddy for him.

Not that Jason had planned on too many outdoor activities. Now that his love for Emma had surfaced he planned on doing even less. He wanted her all to himself. Her desire had been palpable just now. Whether it was for him or just for sex was immaterial at this point in time. Beggars couldn't be choosers. Either way, he aimed to take full advantage of her blossoming sensuality during this coming week, to bind her to him as woman had been bound to man for centuries. With a baby.

He knew for a fact this week was right in the middle of her cycle. She hadn't wanted a period to spoil their wedding day and had chosen a safe date. She'd also said she wanted to try for a baby straight away herself. And why not? In her eyes, this was hardly the love match of the century. It was a marriage made with heads, not hearts. A marriage based on liking and friendship, caring and commitment. Having a family was a natural progression of such a marriage. Months spent just blindly making love simply for the sake of expressing one's love for each other was not on the agenda.

Jason almost groaned aloud at the thought. What he would not give...

'What a pretty place!' Emma exclaimed as they drove into Narooma. 'I love Tindley, but this could become my second most favourite town.'

'Become?'

'We'll have to come back every year to celebrate our anniversary.'

'We haven't celebrated the original yet,' he returned drily, his own frustration beginning to bother him. So many months without sex was enough to bother any man, he reckoned.

'I can't wait to get this dress off,' she said.

'Neither can I,' he muttered, and she laughed.

It broke his tension, that laugh, and he laughed too. Their eyes met and he could have sworn he saw love in hers.

But of course that was just wishful thinking. Still, he could pretend, couldn't he?

'Bags the bathroom first,' he said, and she pouted at him. 'Only joking,' he added. 'The place I booked has two bathrooms.'

'Two! But what for?'

'For impatient people?' he suggested, and she laughed again.

'No,' he explained, 'it's a holiday unit, and most don't come any smaller than two-bedroomed. According to the agent, it also has a fully equipped kitchen, L-shaped lounge-diner, a lock up garage, and a balcony with a view second to none. How does that sound, Mrs Steel?'

'Heavenly,' she said, smiling. 'The unit sounds pretty good, too.'

He almost said it then; he almost opened his mouth and told her he loved her. But he didn't. He didn't dare. She might think he was lying, or trying to emotionally blackmail her, or manipulate her. Better they continue as they were, as good friends and soon-to-be lovers.

'I have to collect the keys from the agency,' he explained when he pulled over to the kerb in the small hilly main street. 'Won't be a minute.'

He dashed in, ignored the stares of the two girls behind the desk, collected the keys and dashed out again. Several other passersby raised their eyebrows as he ran around and jumped into his car. He supposed it wasn't every day they saw a man in a formal black dinner suit dashing about the streets in daylight. But, hell, he was in a hurry.

The unit lived up to the wraps put on it by the travel agent, being very stylish, with great cane furniture and all the mod cons. Air-conditioning. A spa bath in the main bathroom. A huge television and video.

It was one of two units on the second floor of a brand-new block, tucked in behind the shopping centre and overlooking a park, with the small harbour beyond. Further out lay the breakwaters, and then the ocean. The balcony was totally private, with side walls. An outdoor table and two chairs in green iron-work sat in one corner, potted palms in the other.

When Emma slid back the large glass door and wandered out to admire the view, a cool breeze swirled the filmy curtains. Jason stayed inside, watching her and thinking she looked like an angel—or perhaps a ghost—standing out there in her long white dress, its full skirt whipped back by the wind, her fair hair lifting from her pale throat. The pearl choker gleamed in the dusky light, reminding Jason of the first time he'd seen her.

On that occasion her elegantly sensual neck had been enhanced by a gold chain. He recalled wanting to pull her head back with it so he could kiss her. He found the pearl choker infinitely more erotic. Why that was, he wasn't sure. Maybe because it looked like a collar, and evoked images of bondage which appealed to his dark side. He could almost understand why men of yore kidnapped fair damsels and kept them enslaved in dungeons for their pleasure, and theirs alone. There was something deeply primitive about such an action. And deeply arousing.

He'd waited long enough.

'Emma!' he called out sharply, and she whirled around, her hair whipping across her face.

He didn't have to say another word. She came back through the open glass door and slid it shut. Turning, she came to him across the thick blue carpet and slid her arms up around his neck, reaching up on tiptoe till her mouth was a breath away from his.

'Yes?' she whispered, her lips falling softly apart.

He groaned, and took what she offered, all his good intentions of focusing on her pleasure alone disintegrating under the wild passion of her response. For a few mad moments he was hers for the taking, not the other way around. But then she wrenched her mouth away and stepped back from him, flushed and trembling.

When her hands lifted to reach blindly behind her in search of her zipper, he swiftly pulled himself together. He had to take charge of his emotions, take control of the situation, or all would be lost.

'No,' he said firmly, forcibly ignoring his own fierce arousal. 'Let me...'

CHAPTER NINE

HE MOVED behind her and placed his hands on her shoulders, running them down then up her lace-encased arms, feeling her tension, deliberately stoking it as he repeated the action. Only when she trembled did he reach for and pull the zipper slowly down her back, bending at the same time to kiss the small span of flesh between the top of that tantalising necklace and the lobe of her ear. The zipper undone, his lips travelled upwards to that lobe, and then up to her ear, breathing softly into the soft, sensitive well.

'Oh,' she gasped, and a shiver ran down her spine.

He sent his tongue where his breath had been and she shuddered, her head twisting away from him so that his mouth connected with the pearl choker. He resisted the temptation to remove it, choosing instead to peel back her dress and expose her back, her stunningly bare back.

For a few seconds he thought she wasn't wearing a bra, but when he trailed a fingertip down her spine he saw she was actually wearing one of those strapless corsellettes which dipped dangerously down at the back in a deep V, the hooks connecting just above her waist, pulling that waist in tightly, forcing her slender hips to flare out more than her natural body shape.

The corset was white, and made of satin and lace. Boned at the front, no doubt, the kind of exotic, erotic contraption which pushed the breasts up and together, and gave any woman wearer a shape so feminine and desirable that just looking at her was enough to send any red-blooded man's desire meter sky-high.

Jason's was already off the planet. How he was going to control himself here, he had no idea.

Her dress suddenly slipped from his fingers and pooled on the carpet, and his heart jolted at the sight before his eyes. Oh, God! The corset had suspenders, and lacy stockings, and nothing to cover her bottom but a tiny thong of satin between the two most delectable buttocks he'd ever seen.

He turned her to face him, because that was safer. Or he thought it was till he did it, only to find himself confronted with even more torment. Her breasts pouted up at him, erect nipples half escaping the provocative push-up cups. The front was as dangerously cut as the back, lower down displaying an R-rated amount of smoothly shaven flesh. On top of that she was looking up at him with huge liquid eyes, as though he were some Greek God and she his sex slave.

If only she knew. *He* was the slave, not her. He would do anything for her. Anything.

'You are so beautiful,' he murmured, his gaze hot upon her. 'And so incredibly sexy.' He'd mistakenly thought she would never wear provocative underwear. He'd foolishly imagined he would prefer her in flannelette, instead of satin and lace.

Stupid, stupid Jason!

'I had to order it from a catalogue,' she said, blushing wildly. 'It…it only came this week.'

'It's…fantastic.'

'You really like it? I…I hoped you would.'

'I love it.'

'Do…do you want me to take it off?'

'Hell, no,' he said, and pulled her into his arms, kissing her ravenously, sliding his hands down her back to cup her buttocks and press her hard against him. The cool-headed part of him warned him to slow down; the rest ignored any such advice and just did what came naturally.

What came naturally was to pull her down onto the carpet, laying her beneath him as he ravaged her body with his mouth and hands. The flimsy lace cups were no barrier to his desires, easily pushed aside so that his hungry lips could claim the evidence of *her* arousal.

Emma's first gasp was followed by a low moan, then another gasp as he moved over to her other nipple.

The desperate sounds she made only inflamed him further as he licked and sucked both peaks into twin points of exquisite torment. Instinct and experience told him when to move on, breathing hot breaths over her satin-covered stomach while his hands found and unsnapped the press-studs between her legs. He peeled the scraps of material back and bared her to his questing lips. When she gasped and wriggled, he pressed one palm firmly down on her stomach while his other hand stroked her quivering thighs further apart.

He knew exactly what to do, and when to do it, ignoring her one feeble, fluttering protest, taking her swiftly beyond embarrassment to a world which knew no such inhibitions, only the most incredibly addictive compelling pleasure. He felt her surrender to its power, felt her lose herself to a rapidly rising rapture. She struggled for breath, sucking in deeply over and over as her body melted with heat. Her cries were sometimes gasps, sometimes moans.

And then she was really crying out, sobbing and shuddering as everything broke within her, her flesh spasming wildly under the most intense orgasm he'd ever given a woman.

Jason collapsed beside her on the carpet, her pleasure having unexpectedly become his pleasure, shocking him. He'd never known anything like it.

He lay like that for several minutes, before levering himself up on one elbow to look down at her. Her arms were flung out, palms up, by her sides. Her eyes were shut and her lips still agape.

He left her there and made his way into the bathroom, stripping as he went and stepping into the shower. Five minutes later he was back, scooping her up into his arms and carrying her towards the main bedroom.

Her eyes opened on a low moan.

'You're not going to sleep yet, Mrs Steel,' he told her mockingly. 'That was just the entrée. Now we're moving on to the main course.' And, laying her face down in the bed, he proceeded to unhook the corsellete and strip her totally, even dispensing with the pearl choker this time. His movements were swift and impatient, his inadequately subdued flesh already on the rise again. 'Did you think your wifely duties were over for the night?' he asked as he snapped on a bed-side lamp and rolled her over.

'Oh,' she gasped. 'You're naked!'

'And so are you, my lovely,' he said, and climbed onto the bed beside her.

Her blush was charming. But she made no move to cover herself. He propped himself up on one elbow and began to touch wherever his eyes travelled. She had a lovely feminine shape, even without the help of underwear. Breasts just full enough. A tiny waist. Slender hips and thighs. It was her skin, however, which fascinated him, with its satiny softness. Even her pubic hair was soft, curling damply between her legs. He stroked those legs apart once more and watched her while he explored every inch of her body. Her breathing quickened once more. Her eyes closed and her lips fell slightly apart.

His own pulse was racing, but he remained in control. What had happened earlier had calmed him somewhat.

He slipped one finger inside her and her eyes shot open. Again he knew exactly where to touch, searching for and finding that elusive G spot. Her eyes widened and her lips fell further apart on a low moan. He kissed her while one finger eventually became two, then three. She was opening for him, her flesh growing slick and eager. The moment she started grasping and releasing his fingers he stopped kissing her, his head lifting.

Till that moment he'd deliberately avoided thinking of his own arousal, so he was astonished to find he was bigger and harder than he'd ever been in his life. Not good, he thought, but what could he do about it?

'Jason,' she moaned when his hand withdrew.

'It's all right,' he muttered, and levered himself over, between her legs. Straight away she lifted her knees and wrapped her ankles and arms around him. Hell, she was a natural, he thought, as she rocked slightly back and forth, rubbing her moist flesh against him.

His aim was to penetrate her as gently as possible, so as not to hurt her. It was both agony and ecstasy as he eased his aching flesh inside hers, for whilst she was deliciously tight, her sharp intake of breath indicated that he *was* causing her some discomfort. She was tensing up; he could feel. He was losing her.

'Oh, God,' she cried painfully, but he simply could not stop at that point. What good would it have done, anyway?

'I'm sorry,' he rasped, and wondered if it might be better to do this more quickly.

Her resistance was surprising him. He'd thought he'd prepared her well. Or was his extra hardness the trouble? Whatever, his own pleasure at being sheathed inside her was incredible. He'd never felt anything like it. That, combined with the knowledge that she was finally his, that he was one with the woman he loved, broke his control.

He drove in to the hilt.

She didn't cry out. But she seemed stunned, lying motionless beneath him for a while, but then slowly, as he began to move, she came to life beneath him, moving with him, her nails digging into his back. He had her again. Clasping her tighter, Jason thrust harder and deeper.

'Oh,' she cried, but not from pain. From pleasure. He could hear it, feel it. And then she was coming around him, her muscles contracting wildly. He was powerless to last any longer, his seed racing towards her waiting womb, exploding deep within her. His groan was primal, his back arching with the force of his climax. He came and came and came.

Towards the end of his ecstasy, Jason realised his bride was crying, sobbing into his chest with he knew not what emotions. Regret that he wasn't Ratchitt?

Jason's stomach lurched, all pleasure ceasing.

It tore him apart that the reality of what had just happened was too much for her, that in her heart she still wanted Ratchitt. Jealousy ripped through Jason as he imagined she might have responded so intensely because she'd been pretending it was *Ratchitt's* arms around her tonight, *his* mouth pleasuring her, *him* buried deep inside her.

It took every ounce of maturity not to act like some stupid, self-destructive fool. Maybe she would have preferred Ratchitt, but she'd married *him*, hadn't she? He was the man lying in bed with her tonight. He would be the man in her bed every night. The man who would father her children. Ratchitt was the stupid fool!

So he pushed aside his futile thinking and held her to him till she stopped crying and fell asleep. Only then did he slide from underneath her and try to sleep himself. But he remained, wide-eyed and awake, till the wee hours of the morning, thinking of his mother's words once more.

You can't have everything in life, son...

She'd never been so wrong. Or so right.

CHAPTER TEN

JASON woke to a gentle hand on his shoulder.

'What?' he said, sitting bolt upright and almost upsetting the tray Emma was carrying.

She stepped back and stood there, smiling shyly down at him, all dressed and pretty in pale pink. 'It's almost eleven,' she said.

'Good Lord!' He rarely slept in like that.

'I've been up for hours,' she went on. 'Been shopping too, as you can see. There wasn't anything in the cupboards except tea, coffee, sugar and toilet paper. I thought you would need something more substantial than that.' She smiled and bent to place the tray on the bedside table. 'I know you usually have muesli for breakfast, but I didn't think honeymoons were the right occasion for the mundane. I looked for something more decadent. Did I do right?'

His eyes swept over the breakfast tray, with its grapefruit juice, bacon and eggs, fried tomato and sautéed mushrooms. Two slices of perfectly browned toast rested on a bread plate along with a dollop of butter. Two pretty paper serviettes were tucked underneath.

'You did very right,' he said, levering himself up to sit back against the headboard, careful to arrange the sheet over him so she wouldn't be embarrassed by his nudity. He could see the morning had brought back some of her ingrained innocence. The sensual partner of the night before had been put to bed, and in her place was the Emma he'd first met. A little shy. A little prim. A lot old-fashioned.

He was dying to go to the bathroom, but decided that could wait till she was gone. 'This is fantastic, Emma. You shouldn't have.'

'But of course I should! You're my husband.'

Something squeezed tight within him. He wasn't sure if it was satisfaction, or the beginnings of despair. Was that all he would ever be to her, her husband?

Probably, he decided, and tried not to look wretched. At least she couldn't claim last night had been for duty alone. She'd enjoyed it, even if she *had* cried afterwards.

Jason decided not to cry for the moon himself. He'd made the decision to marry with his head, and not his heart. Well, that was what he'd got. A wife who'd married *him* with her head and not her heart. He should be thankful she found pleasure in his body.

That was if it *was his* body she was finding pleasure in.

'I'll bring your coffee in a little while,' she said sweetly. 'Meanwhile, I'll unpack your clothes.'

'No!' he jumped in, quite sharply, and she looked alarmed. 'No, I don't want you to do that, Emma,' he went on more calmly. 'Look, I don't know what that aunt of yours brought you up to think a wife should be, but I don't expect you to be my maid. I can look after myself very well. I can look after my own clothes too. I can even wash and iron with the best of them. Not that I have to, in the main. I have a woman come in Mondays and Thursdays who takes care of that, plus the general cleaning. You know her. Joanne Hatfield. She's a single mum and can do with the money. I have no intention of letting her go just because I'm married now.'

Emma didn't seem to know what to make of his speech, looking confused and distressed.

'I married you for *you*, Emma,' he insisted, 'not to get a free housekeeper. Of course, I don't mind if you cook, since you're so good at it, but I'll be doing the washing-up every night.'

She looked horrified. 'I can't let you do that. I mean…what would everyone think?'

'I don't give a stuff what they think. You said you were going to go on working in the sweet shop. Working couples share the chores these days.'

'But you'll be working much longer hours than me some days.'

His smile was soft. She really was very sweet. 'Then on those days I'll let you spoil me and wash up as well, okay?'

Her smile was uncertain. 'If you say so…'

'I say so. Now…what would you like to do today?'

Jason was startled when her gaze instinctively moved over his naked chest, then over the rumpled bedclothes. Her cheeks were pink by the time her eyes lifted back to his. 'I don't really know,' she said, but her face told a different story. She wanted to spend

the day in bed with him. She was just not bold enough
to say so. 'Anything you like,' she added.

Anything he liked...

Now that was an invitation no man could turn
down, let alone one in love with the lovely young
woman making the offer. Any spoiling thoughts about
Ratchitt were firmly pushed aside in favour of the
reality of the moment, which was that Emma desired
him. *Him.* Her husband.

But there were things he had do first. Breakfast.
The bathroom. But after that...after that he'd do what
she wanted. And how!

'Give me half an hour,' he said, his eyes holding
hers. 'Then we'll see what I can come up with.'

'Darn!' Jason exclaimed, and sat up abruptly in bed.
'I forgot to do something.'

Emma glanced up at him. 'I can't think what,' she
said in all seriousness. 'Is there anything else?'

He grinned, then dropped a kiss on her pretty pink
mouth. 'That's for me to know and you to find out.'
They'd been making love on and off all day. At least,
Jason had been making love to *Emma* on and off all
day, and he had no intention of changing that formula
at this stage. He certainly wasn't going to urge her to
take the reins where lovemaking was concerned, not
even in foreplay. He definitely shrank from suggesting
she manually or orally arouse him. Whilst he enjoyed
both activities a lot, he knew some girls never took
to doing either, and he didn't want to risk repulsing
Emma this early in their marriage. She was so re-

sponsive when he made love to her. Silly to spoil things by asking for more than she was ready to give.

There was plenty of time to become adventurous later in their marriage, he reasoned sensibly.

Besides, he didn't want another Adele, did he? He wanted his innocent and inexperienced Emma, who gained the most intense satisfaction from the simplest of lovemaking. He glanced at her now, with the sheet modestly pulled up over her bare breasts, her face still slightly flushed from her last orgasm.

'You stay right there,' he said as he scrambled out of bed. But when he walked round to the foot of the bed, where he was sure he'd dropped his clothes, they weren't there! 'Now where is that darned dinner jacket of mine?'

'Oh…I…er…hung it up. Before you asked me not to,' she added swiftly. 'It was lying on the floor, along with all your other things.'

He glared at her in mock exasperation, then laughed. 'You're forgiven. Where did you hang it?'

She nodded towards the wardrobe door on the right. He dived in and quickly retrieved the dark green velvet box, hiding it behind his back as he turned to face her.

'What are you hiding?' she asked eagerly.

'Not much,' he countered wryly, glancing down at his naked self with its surprisingly semi-aroused equipment. When he looked back up he was touched to see she was blushing. Not once, in all the years he'd been with Adele, had he ever seen that woman blush. He doubted she knew how.

Emma smiled. 'Stop embarrassing me and tell me what you have there.'

'Shall I bring it over to you?'

'Yes,' she said, then added impishly, 'All of it!'

'You saucy minx!'

'If I am, then you're to blame,' she accused. 'You make me think things and want to do things I've never wanted to do before.'

Jason liked the sound of that. 'Tell me more,' he said, and came over to sit on the side of the bed.

'Only after you've shown me what you have behind your back.'

'It's a deal.' And he produced the green velvet box. 'I meant to give you this on our wedding night. But I got waylaid by a wanton lady in wicked white suspenders.'

She frowned down at the box, then up at him. 'It looks like a ring...'

'Why don't you open it and find out for sure?'

She did, gasping at the sight of the diamond-and emerald-encrusted band. 'Oh, Jason, it's lovely! Why, it matches my engagement ring exactly.'

'That was the idea.' He took it from the box and slid it on her finger.

'And it fits exactly!' she exclaimed delightedly.

'It's called an eternity ring,' he explained. 'Which means you're mine now, Emma...for ever and ever.'

She touched the ring as though it were the most precious thing in the world. 'For ever and ever,' she murmured, before looking up, her eyes clouding a little. 'That's a long time, Jason.'

His heart lurched, but he kept his face steady. 'For ever with you won't be long enough, my darling girl,' he whispered, and, bending, kissed her tenderly on the lips.

When his head lifted, her eyes were swimming.

'If you cry again,' he warned, wagging his finger at her, 'I will have to take stern measures.'

She smiled through her tears. 'Such as what?'

'Such as making you stay in bed with me for the rest of the day.'

'Oh, dear. Such a terrible punishment.'

Jason loved the way her lips started twitching as she struggled not to laugh or smile. She had a wicked little sense of humour at times. He'd found that out when they'd watched movies together.

He kept a straight face himself with great difficulty. 'Wives must be taught their place, right from the word go!'

'And where is that?'

'Under their husbands, of course. So tell me, wife,' he said, deliberately keeping things light and teasing, 'what are these wicked things I make you think of and want to do?'

Her eyes slid away, and the colour zoomed back into her cheeks. 'I…I don't like to say…'

'Emma, darling, there should be no secrets between husbands and wives, especially in the bedroom. Tell me. I won't be shocked.'

She opened her mouth, then closed it again, shaking her head. 'Oh, I simply can't.'

'Of course you can. I'm a doctor.' And he grinned at her.

'This is serious, Jason!'

'No, it's not, Emma. Not always. Sex can be fun too, you know. The trouble is people get all uptight about it. Like you did before our wedding. They wonder and worry too much. If you want me to do something, or vice versa, then you must say so. I know it can be a bit difficult, but once you've expressed your desires out loud the first time, you'll find it easier the next time. Try it. Tell me one thing you want to do. Just one thing.'

She stared at him, then visibly swallowed. 'All right...I'll try...' Her eyes shifted from his, and her cheeks glowed pink. 'Sometimes,' she said huskily, 'when I look at you, I...I want to touch you so badly. Like now...with you sitting there like that...I want to reach out and...and...'

He could see her courage was failing her, so he took her hand and placed it in his lap. Her soft fingers rested against his semi-erect penis. 'Oh!' she gasped, staring down at him as it began to swell further. Carefully, gently, he moved her hand so that she was stroking the rapidly lengthening shaft. Without being told, she suddenly encircled it totally with her hand and exerted a wonderful pressure.

He could not help it. He groaned. Her hand froze and her eyes flew up, their expression a mixture of confusion and fascination.

'Did I hurt you?'

'God, no,' he rasped. 'Keep going.'

'I...don't really know what to do.'

'You're doing wonderfully.'

'It...it feels lovely,' she whispered, once he was fully erect. 'So strong and smooth. And this bit is like satin...'

He sucked in a sharp breath when her fingertips grazed over the head. Her eyes came up again, and this time they were knowing upon him. 'You like that, don't you?' she murmured as she repeated the action over and over.

He must have choked out something.

'Tell me what else you like?' she insisted.

Jason was tempted, but he knew it was too soon. Besides, he was fast reaching the point of no return. So he whisked her hand away and whipped her under him on the bed. 'This,' he growled, and surged deep inside her. 'This is what I like.'

The week went quickly, but perfectly. Jason could not have been happier. Emma was everything he'd already known she was, and everything he'd hoped she'd be. Giving and loving, warm and quite wonderful. And that was *out* of bed.

In bed, she was just so beautiful, and flatteringly insatiable for him. Soon, she seemed to want him as much as he wanted her, and that was saying something, since he wanted her all the time. All those wonderful holiday activities Narooma was famous for swiftly went by the board in favour of traditional honeymoon activities. They did leave the unit to dine each evening, and they did sleep for a few hours each night, and sometimes during the afternoon, but that was about it. The rest of the time was spent making love.

On their last afternoon, Emma insisted on a visit to the golf course. 'You told me last week how much you were looking forward to playing a round here. Besides,' she added, 'I'd like to learn to play myself. Do you think you could teach me?'

Jason was surprised. Most young women didn't care for golf at all. 'Sure I could, but do you really want to play?'

'Married couples should do things together,' she stated simply. ''Whither thou goest, I will go'.'

Jason liked the image of togetherness this projected, but not the reference to the dutiful wife, Ruth, in the Bible. Emma's penchant for duty rather irked him when applied to their personal relationship. He wanted her to do things with him because she enjoyed them, never because she thought it was her job. 'You should only play golf if you really enjoy the game, Emma.'

Her frown was thoughtful. 'I suppose so,' she agreed, then flashed him a sweet smile. 'But how will I know I enjoy something if I don't try it?'

Jason could not complain about the logic in that. 'Fair enough. Do you have any clothes suitable for golf with you? You can't play in a dress.'

'Will shorts and T-shirt do?'

'Fine. What about on your feet? You can't wear sandals. They'll slip.'

'I have some sandshoes.'

'They'll do. For now. But if you like the game I'll buy you some proper golf shoes.'

'I can afford to buy my own shoes,' she said, then hurried off to dress, leaving Jason to throw a rueful look after her. What a contradiction in terms she was sometimes! Wanting to be an old-fashioned wife to him, yet at the same maintaining a very modern financial independence.

Jason wasn't sure if he liked either, which was perverse. What was not to like?

Emma was a bit quiet on the drive to the golf course, her face turned away from him. She might have been admiring the scenery—the view of the blue Pacific beyond the emerald-green fairways *was* spectacular—but he had a feeling her mind was a million miles away.

'Is there anything wrong, darling?' he asked softly, after he'd parked the car and she was still sitting there, totally unaware that they'd come to a standstill and he'd turned off the engine. Her head jerked round, a stiff smile hiding whatever emotion she'd swiftly wiped from her face.

'No. Not really. It was just thinking…we have to go back tomorrow, and I…I can't say I want to.'

Jason sighed with relief. So *that* was it! She didn't want their honeymoon to end. An understandable reaction, but nothing to worry about. For a moment there…

He reached out to lay a gentle hand against her cheek. 'I know how you feel,' he murmured. 'It would be lovely to stay here for ever, wouldn't it? Just you and me and no one else.'

Her hand came up to cover his and she leant her cheek into his palm. 'Yes,' she said simply, and looked deep into his eyes, her smile soft and full of tenderness. Jason's body immediately began to ache for her again.

'Time for golf, I think,' he said, and abruptly withdrew his hand, turning his head away.

Teaching Emma to play golf was a welcome distraction. So was her aptitude for the game. 'You're going to be a handy little player with some practice,' he complimented her when they were well into the second nine.

'But I've lost nearly all of your balls!' she wailed. 'Two in the ocean and three in that awful lake back there!' And she pointed angrily at the wide water hazard now behind them, her face still flushed with frustration. Stubborn by nature, she'd been determined to hit over it and not around, and three times her ball had gone to a watery grave.

'There are worse things in the world, Emma,' he commiserated, 'than lost balls. I still have two left; one for you and one for me.'

She stared at him, then burst out laughing. Only then did he realise what he'd said, and he grinned. 'Yes...well, shall we call it a day and go home?'

'No fear! I'm determined to finish. And to get better.'

'You're darned good for a beginner already.'

Her surprised pleasure touched him. Hadn't anyone ever told her how good she was at anything before?

'Really?' she asked.

'Really.'

'I suppose I've always been pretty good at doing things with my hands.'

'Mmm. So I've noticed,' he murmured.

Her blush was instantaneous, her gaze skittering away from his. Jason could not help but smile. When her eyes returned to his, he was surprised to see they carried a slight frown. Her mouth opened to say something, then shut again.

'What?' he queried.

More colour, but this time she held his gaze and spoke. 'You once told me I shouldn't be scared to tell you anything…or ask you anything… About sex, that is.'

Jason tried not to look surprised, or alarmed. 'That's right.'

'What you said just now about my being good with my hands… I've been thinking… I mean… Oh, dear, this is difficult.' And she glanced around to see if anyone was nearby. There wasn't, the back nine of the course almost deserted at this late hour in the afternoon.

Jason waited patiently for her to get over her embarrassment and continue.

She bit her bottom lip and refused to look at him, instead finding a target for her eyes somewhere on the grass before going on in halting whispers. 'I've been wondering…why you haven't asked me…to…um… do *more*…in bed.'

'More?' Jason repeated a little numbly while his heart raced. 'What, exactly, do you mean?' he asked.

Her eyes swung to his, glittering now within their bright pink setting. She'd never looked so embarrassed, or so incredibly desirable. 'Oh, Jason, please don't make me spell it out. You must know what I mean. You're an experienced lover. And, while I'm not, I *have* read all those magazine articles which go on about the things men most like in bed. There's one especially, which crops up all the time. I've been wondering why you haven't asked me to do…that. You said I was to always ask for things I wanted. Why haven't you? Wouldn't you like me to…to do that to you?'

Her questions flustered him almost as much as they were flustering her. 'I…well…yes, of course I would. But I didn't think you'd want to. I mean…women usually only do that when they…er…um…'

'When they're madly in love with their partner?' she finished for him.

'I guess so,' he agreed uncomfortably, although he'd been going to say when they'd been having sex a little longer than a week.

'What about wives? Wouldn't wives generally do it for their husbands?'

'Emma, I don't feel comfortable with this conversation.'

'Why not?'

He was beginning to get irritated. *Why not?*

Because it smacked of the same thing as her wanting to unpack his clothes and iron his shirts and bring him breakfast in bed. He didn't want her thinking she *had* to do things like that, just because she was married to him. Fellatio was not part of her job description as his wife!

'Did Adele do it?' she demanded to know.

Hell, what was he going to say to that?

'Not often,' he mumbled.

'Did you like it when she did?'

Hell on earth! *'Yes,'* he bit out.

'Then I want to do it too,' she said stubbornly. 'I want to do everything you like. Do you understand me, Jason? I want to.'

He understood, only too well. And, while it pained him, he knew he'd be too weak to say no.

Besides, he thought with a bitterly ironic twist on what she'd said earlier, how did he know she wouldn't enjoy it, if he didn't let her try?

CHAPTER ELEVEN

JASON woke to an empty bed. Light was filtering in through the curtains, but it felt early. Rolling over, he picked up his watch from the bedside table and looked at the time. Only ten past five.

He glanced around, looking for Emma. The *en suite* bathroom door was wide open. She wasn't in there. Possibly she'd gone to the toilet in the main bathroom, so as not to wake him. That was the sort of sweet thing Emma would do.

The memory of her last night, however, did not conjure up thoughts of sweetness so much, but the most incredible passion. She'd been shy at first, though clearly determined. Any worry Jason had had over how he might react to such an intimacy was soon obliterated. He'd been so turned on he'd ended up demanding all she had to give. And more!

He hoped he hadn't shocked her.

She hadn't seemed shocked. She'd curled up to him afterwards like a cat who'd licked up all the cream, a purring, contented cat. Yet now she was gone from the bed, when she should have been still beside him, sleeping the sleep of the sated.

Throwing back the covers, Jason walked, nude, out into the living room. A pre-dawn glow was shining through the open glass doors and onto the blue carpet, the rectangle of light broken only by the figure on the balcony. Emma was standing there, leaning against the railing, watching the sun rise, wearing his navy silk bathrobe.

His mouth was creasing into a relieved smile when, suddenly, her head dropped into her hands and her shoulders began to shake.

Appalled, Jason rushed across the room and wrenched open the glass door. With a strangled sob, she whirled, and he saw the devastation in her face. The utter, utter devastation.

'My God, Emma,' he cried. 'What is it? What's wrong?'

'Oh, Jason!' She was shaking her head and crying at the same time.

He came forward and took her in his arms, oblivious of the cool dawn air pricking his skin into goose bumps. 'Tell me,' he insisted.

'I don't know how to,' she choked out, and buried her face into his chest.

He put a finger under her wobbly chin and lifted it so that she had to look him straight in the eye, even though hers were flooded.

'You must tell me what's wrong, Emma. You can't cry like this without telling me what's the matter.'

'It...it's Dean,' she confessed, bravely blinking back the tears. 'He's back.'

His hands dropped away from her face as though stung. 'Back? What do you mean, back? You mean in Tindley?'

She nodded, her eyes wide and frightened.

Confusion warred with apprehension within Jason. 'How could you possibly know that?' he asked. 'Did someone ring here during the night? Did you ring someone in Tindley?'

She shook her head. 'No.'

'Then make sense, damn you,' he snapped, and she flinched. He hadn't meant to swear at her, but God in heaven, he was only human. His worst nightmare was happening and he couldn't even get a handle on it.

'He...he came back the day of the wedding,' she said on a raw whisper, fear still in her face.

Jason was staggered. 'On the day of our wedding? When? Where? Where did you see him?'

'Please, let's go inside. I don't want to discuss this out here.' And she bolted from the balcony into the living room. He followed, slamming the glass door shut behind him.

'You *saw* him, didn't you?' he flung at her, and she flinched again. Oh, yes, she'd seen him, he suddenly realised. Nothing short of a personal visit could have rattled her like this.

And then the penny dropped, and a chill rippled through him.

'You don't have to say anything,' he said coldly. 'I get the picture. He showed up at your place just before the wedding. That's why you were late at the church. So what did he want? As if I don't know!'

'Oh, Jason, please don't be like that! Oh, God, this was what I was afraid of all this week. How you would react.'

'You should have told me, Emma.'

'When? When could I have told you without spoiling our wedding, and then our honeymoon? I wanted

to give us a chance to start right. I didn't want you
to…to…'

'To what? To know you were thinking of Ratchitt
every time I made love to you? To worry that you
might have married me just because you thought it
was the right thing to do, or because you didn't have
the guts to call the wedding off at the last moment?
You haven't done me any favours, Emma, marrying
me when your heart is breaking over another man.
Which reminds me, just who *were* you going down
on last night? Me, or Ratchitt?'

Her hand cracked across his face with such suddenness and such force that he reeled backwards, staring at her as his hand came up to gingerly touch his
stinging cheek. Her look of indignant outrage might
have convinced someone else, but not him, not when
his stomach was reeling at the thought of the way her
eyes had always closed last night, every time she'd
taken him into her mouth.

'How dare you say that to me?' she exclaimed, her
voice shaking. 'I chose to marry *you*, not Dean. What
I told you in the car after the wedding was the truth.
Yes, Dean came and asked me not to marry you but
to marry him instead. I said no. I chose you, Jason. I
did what you told me to do. Made the decision not to
choose a partner who was wrong for me. When Dean
came back after all this time, I began to see him as
I'd never seen him before. He swaggered in, all macho selfishness, explaining nothing, caring about nobody but himself. It didn't bother him that he might
be spoiling our wedding day. He was simply intent

on grabbing what he wanted with no thought for anyone else but himself.'

'And did he?'

'Did he what?'

'Grab you?'

'Yes, he grabbed me. And he kissed me. He even told me he still loved me.'

'Did you believe him?'

'As you said, if he really loved me he'd have come back sooner. Dean arrogantly thought I'd still be waiting for him. He thought I'd still be in love with him.'

'And are you, Emma?'

'I don't know, Jason. I honestly don't know. All I can say is I'm not blind to him any more. And I don't want to marry him any more. I'm not sorry I married you. Not for a moment.'

A few seconds' elation was soon replaced by what Emma had left unsaid. She might not want to marry Ratchitt, but that didn't mean she didn't still want him. Jason could not get out of his mind the way her mouth had been totally devoid of lipstick at their wedding. That had taken a lot of kissing.

'Did you like it when Ratchitt kissed you?' he asked, sounding quite calm. But inside he was churning.

She could not meet his eyes, and he knew the truth.

Jason wanted to kill them both. 'So what was the outcome? What did he say to you when you knocked him back again? And I want the truth, Emma. No prevarications, and no watered-down words. What, exactly, did he say?'

'He...he said I was welcome to marry you, but that

one day we would be together, and nothing and nobody could stop that, certainly not some stupid fool of a husband I didn't even love.'

'Really? And how did he know that you didn't love me? Could it be because of the way you kissed him back?'

She went bright red. 'I didn't mean to, Jason. It was like I was in shock, or on auto-pilot, or hypnotised. When he pulled me into his arms, for one mad moment it was just like it used to be. I forgot…everything. By the time I woke up to reality, he was smiling smugly down at me. I…I wiped my mouth so many times after he was gone, you've no idea. I can assure you, Jason, that when you kissed me in the church that day, I…I liked it just as much.'

'Good God, am I supposed to be grateful for that?' He was shaking his head at her, fearing that he'd been right all along. She'd spent her entire honeymoon thinking of Ratchitt, trying her heart out to be a good wife, but wondering in the back of her mind if it might have been better with him.

His sigh carried defeat. 'I don't know what to say to you.'

'Tell me you you're glad I chose to marry you. Tell me you care about me. Tell me you trust me!'

'Hard for a husband to trust his wife when she's in love with another man, don't you think?'

'You knew that when you married me.'

Jason's mouth curled into a bitter little smile. 'True. I thought I could handle it when he was a mythical person. A memory. It's slightly different now that he's a real live man living in our town and vowing he won't rest till he seduces my wife!'

'He won't succeed in that, Jason.'

'Oh? Pardon me if I don't feel too confident of that. From what I've heard, Ratchitt would run rings around Casanova himself in the lovemaking department.'

'I wouldn't know about that,' she muttered.

'But you'd like to, wouldn't you?' he accused nastily, jealousy a festering sore in his heart. 'I'll bet you wished you hadn't been Miss Purity a year ago. I'll bet you wish you'd let him do what he wanted back then.'

'Yes, I do, in a way,' she confessed, totally blowing him away. 'But not in the way you think. Look, you've always wanted to know about my relationship with Dean. Maybe it's time I told you.'

'Maybe it is!'

'All right, then,' she snapped, green eyes flashing. 'But not till you've put something on. I can't stand here talking to you when you're in the nude. It's too…distracting.'

Jason didn't know whether to feel flattered or furious. Arching his eyebrows, he strode down to the bathroom where he wrapped a blue bathsheet around his hips. 'This do?' he asked caustically on returning.

'A bit better,' she said agitatedly, and walked over into the compact U-shaped kitchen. 'I think I'll make us some coffee while I talk.'

'Do that,' he bit out, and climbed up on one of the kitchen stools at the small breakfast bar.

She didn't say anything till the electric kettle was

on, and the mugs were all ready, then she turned to face him across the counter.

'I first became infatuated with Dean when I was twelve and he was seventeen. I was in my first year at high school, and he was in his last. Practically every girl in school was mad about him. He was just so sexy-looking and so...oh, I don't know. Dangerous, I guess. He did things other people didn't dare to do. He was always being hauled up in front of the principal. He was labelled a troublemaker, but back then he just seemed exciting. As the years went by he seemed even more exciting, and highly unattainable. He went off to Sydney for ages, then came back riding a motorbike. You know the type. He had an earring in one ear, a tattoo on his arm. He wore tight jeans and a sinful-looking black leather jacket.'

Jason could not believe Emma could have been taken in by such superficial garbage! Till he thought of his relationship with Adele. When had he ever done more than scrape the surface of her personality? He'd been attracted to the glamorous façade, and her animal sensuality. How could he blame Emma for finding Ratchitt attractive when *he'd* been guilty of a similarly shallow infatuation?

But couldn't she see that was all it was? Not love, but the combination of misguided hero-worship and sexual attraction.

A dangerous combination, though. He did concede that.

'But it wasn't just what he looked like,' she went on. 'He had a way of focusing his attention on you sometimes which made you feel so...desirable. And he used to say things. Sneaky little compliments whispered in your ear which made you feel wickedly sexy. Not just to me, of course. He said things like that to any female he fancied. I used to watch him with other girls and ache to have him ask me out. But I didn't think I was his type. Oh, he would flirt with me sometimes, but that was as far as it went. When he finally asked me out, I nearly died. I just couldn't handle it. I lost my head over him. I admit it.'

'Not enough to sleep with him, though?' Jason pointed out testily. He had to say something to bring this paragon of rampant sexuality and charismatic machismo down to size!

Emma sighed. 'You have no idea how hard that was.'

Jason had a pretty good idea how hard it had been for Ratchitt, if Emma had been as responsive to him as she'd been this past week. Not that he had any sympathy for Dean Ratchitt. Hopefully, some day soon, some jealous husband or boyfriend would do the world a favour and castrate the creep!

'I know you think I didn't sleep with Dean because of my old-fashioned stance about sex before marriage,' she elaborated, 'but that had nothing to do with it. Oh, yes, Aunt Ivy did bring me up to think that way, but that's not the real reason I held out. I wanted to go to bed with him like mad. But I was afraid if I did, he'd lose interest in me, as he always lost interest in every female he slept with. I thought keeping him dangling was my only chance to get him to marry me. Which was what I wanted at the time.'

Jason thought he did well to sit there and listen to

his wife tell him of the extraordinary lengths she'd gone to to get Ratchitt to marry her.

'Is that why you didn't sleep with me?' he couldn't resist asking, his voice scornful. 'Because you were afraid I wouldn't marry you if you did?' He didn't imagine that for a moment. He didn't rate such measures.

Strangely, she looked guilty as hell. 'No. I...I stupidly believed that if I hadn't let Dean make love to me this side of marriage, then no way was I going to let someone who...who...'

'Whom you didn't love,' he sneered.

'Oh, that sounds terrible! And it's not how I feel now. I mean...'

'Don't go saying you love me, Emma,' he snapped, 'just because you think you've hurt my feelings! Let's go on as we began, for pity's sake, and not pretend. We went into this marriage with our heads firmly screwed on. Don't let a week of sex confuse you. Not that it wasn't fantastic sex. I have to give credit where credit is due, Emma. How you kept your virginity with Ratchitt is a damned miracle. I just hope that now you don't have any virginity to protect you, your resistance to him finds a new reason.'

'I would never be unfaithful to you, Jason.'

'Are you sure, Emma? Are you sure it won't eat into you that you can still have Ratchitt if you want to. I know human nature. I have an awful feeling that in the end you'll be compelled to turn your romantic fantasies into reality. After all, how would I ever know? There'd be no physical proof now, Emma, just as there wasn't any proof with me and Adele.'

She drew herself up straight, shooting him a proud, yet hurt look. 'You'll just have to trust me, won't you? As I trusted you with that woman. I repeat, Jason, I married you, not Dean. I don't regret that. Not for a moment.'

'Is that why you cried on our wedding night?' he flung at her. 'Because you weren't regretting it was me in your bed and not Ratchitt?'

'My crying that night had nothing to do with Dean.'

'Then what did it have to do with?'

'With you,' she said. 'And me. With our being married and making love on our wedding night and not being in love. I thought that was rather…sad. I guess I *am* a silly romantic at heart. It took me a while to come to terms with the sort of marriage I'd agreed to. But I don't find it sad now, Jason. I think it's fine. Just fine. *More* than fine.'

She was trying to be conciliatory. But the word 'fine' was lukewarm at best. Being the person she was, Emma would continue to try to be a good wife to him, but the reality of her emotions hadn't changed. She would never forget Ratchitt, and never fall in love with *him*.

Which meant she would always be vulnerable to Ratchitt's attentions. If the creep hung around long enough, it was inevitable that one day—perhaps when their marriage was going through a bad patch—she would surrender to her unrequited passion for him. Then where would that leave him?

'Fine,' he bit out, and, whirling, stalked from the room.

He was in the shower when she came into the bathroom and stood outside the shower recess, staring at him through the glass.

'I do not want Dean like I want *you*, Jason. Haven't I shown you that this last week?'

A type of fury ripped through him. A fury born of fear and frustration, a fury rooted in his male ego and sexuality, in everything that had gone before and everything he feared might happen in the future.

He shot back the shower glass and grabbed her nearest wrist, yanking her into the shower with him. The jets of hot water plastered the silk robe around her body, revealing every curve and dip in her body. He didn't remove it, just wrenched it apart, then gobbled in her wet nakedness till he was fully erect. She gasped when he pried her legs apart and pushed up into her where she stood.

He didn't know if she was ready for him or not. There was too much water streaming down over their bodies to tell. Perversely, he didn't want her to be ready, or to find pleasure in his body. He wanted to use her, as men once used their wives of old, without asking permission, without having to care about their satisfaction.

How much of what had happened this week had been real? he agonised as he pumped up into her. And how much was pretence? Since she didn't love him, then what did it matter either way, as long as she let him do what he wanted, whenever he wanted it? She'd made her bed and now she was going to have to lie in it.

Except when the place of copulation was a shower, he thought bitterly. Then she could stand. His eyes flashed to hers and his thoughts were venomous. Why aren't you coming, wife? What's wrong with you this time? Not thinking of Ratchitt enough?

No sooner had this last thought intruded than she closed her eyes with a raw moan, sliding her arms up around his neck, reaching up on tiptoe and urging him on to a more powerful rhythm. Swearing, he hoisted her up off the floor, turning her and pressing her up against the tiles for better support. He hated her when her legs wrapped voluptuously around him, when her mouth gasped wide, when she came with the sort of violent contractions that could *not* have been faked.

It crossed his mind as he shuddered into her that *he* was the one being used here, not the other way around.

CHAPTER TWELVE

'JASON,' she said sternly. 'We *have* to talk.'

He looked up at her from where he'd been eating the mouth-watering casserole she'd served up to him fifteen minutes earlier and which he'd been eating in a brooding silence.

They'd been back at Tindley for ten days, and during that time their marriage had gone from bad to worse. He knew it was mostly his fault, but he couldn't seem to help it. His jealousy of Ratchitt was poisoning his love for her, making him surly and suspicious.

Their sex life had changed considerably since that last tempestuous time in the shower at Narooma. He still made love to her every night, but selfishly and savagely, uncaring if she came or not.

But she always did.

He began to hate her for that. He would have preferred her not to, so that he could imagine she was finding satisfaction elsewhere. His insecurities were beginning to feed upon themselves, and every day he wallowed in all sorts of disgusting scenarios where Ratchitt and his darling wife were concerned.

The worst had seemed to become concrete that very day when he'd gone into the bakery to get his lunch, and Muriel had given him an almost pitying look, followed by a most uncustomary lack of conversation.

'I don't know if should tell you this,' she'd finally said when she handed over his change, 'but Dean's been droppin' in at the sweet shop every time you go out of town on your rounds. I'm not spyin' on Emma, mind, but it's hard not to hear that bike of Dean's. It's very noisy. I…I just thought you'd like to know, Dr Steel. I'm sorry.'

He'd thanked Muriel politely, saying not to worry, he'd handle Dean Ratchitt.

Muriel had still looked worried.

Jason looked at Emma now across the dining-room table and knew his face was closed and cold. He wondered sourly if she was about to come clean, to confess all. Somehow he doubted it. Adultery was much more fun when kept secret and hidden.

'What's there to talk about?'

'I'm not pregnant,' she said. 'My period came today.'

His disappointment was fierce, as was his simmering fury. 'So?'

She winced at the word. 'I think it might be a good idea if I went on the pill for a while.'

'Oh, you do, do you?'

'Yes.'

'Why?'

'Because I don't think I want to bring a baby into this marriage yet.'

'Wise woman,' he said caustically. 'Husbands have a natural aversion to supporting other men's children.'

She looked terribly hurt. 'Oh, Jason… Don't…'

'Don't what? Don't face the truth? You think I don't know about Ratchitt dropping into the shop all the time? Parks his bike out the front and bowls up whenever I'm out of town, so Muriel tells me.'

'I didn't ask him to, Jason, if that's what you're thinking.'

'You have no idea what I'm thinking,' he snapped.

'I have a pretty good idea. But you're wrong. He only stays a few minutes. He just says the same old thing, then leaves.'

'Which is?'

'That he still loves me and he's there for me, when and if I ever need him.'

'In that case, why didn't you tell me?'

'I…I didn't want you thinking things,' she said wretchedly.

A memory shot out of the past, of his doing and saying exactly the same thing when he'd had that encounter with Adele. Emma had trusted him then, but he couldn't seem to find it in his heart to trust her. Perhaps because he loved her so much, and he knew she didn't love him back.

He put down his fork and pushed his plate away. 'Sorry,' he bit out. 'I don't feel hungry tonight. I think I'll go read a book. Don't wait up. I have a feeling I'll be very late to bed.'

'Jason, please don't leave me alone tonight.'

'Sorry, darling, no can do. You have your period, remember? Or were you think of offering me some other service in lieu of the real thing?'

'Why are you doing this?' she cried.

'What?'

'Spoiling everything. I...I can't go on like this.'

'Can't you? And what do you intend doing about it?'

'I don't know.'

'Let me know when you do.'

He whirled and walked out the room, beginning the worst week of his life. She didn't speak to him. Not once. Not a word. Every night she lay next to him in bed like a corpse, and he dared not even put his arm around her. Every morning she set out his breakfast before silently leaving to go to the shop. Every evening she cooked his meal, and even did the washing up, perhaps because she didn't want to ask him to.

And every other day Ratchitt called in at the sweet shop, according to Muriel.

The tension in the house grew till Jason knew he had to say something.

But she beat him to it.

'I've decided what I'm going to do about it,' she said abruptly as the evening meal drew to its usual silent end. 'I'm going to stay at the shop for a while. In my old room.'

He stared at her, his guts in instant turmoil. She was leaving him. Less than a month into their marriage and she was leaving him. A dark suspicion formed in his jealousy-ridden mind when he realised her period would have finished about now.

'How convenient for Ratchitt.'

His snarled remark brought a look of despair. 'You

once said I'd be miserable married to Dean,' she told him bleakly. 'You promised to make me happy. I'm not happy, Jason. I'm more miserable than I've ever been in all my life.'

'I see.'

'Oh, no, Jason. You don't see at all, but I'm not about to explain. You'll only say more nasty things. You have a cruel streak in you, you know. And there I was, when I married you, thinking you were perfect.'

She stood up, and looked him straight in the eye. 'The washing up's yours tonight. And so is everything else till you come to your senses, Jason. I'm not leaving you. Not permanently. I take my marriage vows seriously. But you have to know I won't put up with this. Think about things, and when you want to talk— I mean *really* talk, not throw around useless accusations—then I'll come back. Meanwhile, you can abuse yourself instead of abusing me! As for food, I'm sure Muriel can always provide you with something to eat at night. Or Nancy, or any of the other women in town who still think the sun shines out of your bum! I know better!'

She spun on her heels and walked out on him. He just sat there for a long while, thinking about what she'd said, guilt consuming him over his abominable treatment of her. He knew in his heart she hadn't been unfaithful to him. Emma would not do that. If she was going to go with Ratchitt, she'd say so first. But that didn't mean the creep wasn't waiting in the wings, watching for his chance.

And he was about to get a big fat one, with Emma having moved out.

Finally, he jumped to his feet. What in hell was wrong with him? What was he doing letting someone like Ratchitt ruin his marriage? He should be fighting for his woman, not giving another man every chance to steal her away from him.

And 'fighting' was the operative word! Men like Ratchitt didn't understand polite conversation. They needed to have a fist shoved down their throats before they took any notice. Jason hadn't been brought up in the outer Western suburbs of Sydney for nothing. He might *seem* like a civilised man on the surface, with an educated voice and fancy clothes, but underneath he was still the same streetwise kid who'd had to stand up for himself with his fists more times than he could count.

Time for action. Time to bring things down to Ratchitt's level. Snatching up his car keys, he stormed from the house, slamming the door behind him.

Jason knew where he lived. He'd paid a house call to his cantankerous old man.

In took ten minutes to cover the distance from Tindley to the run-down old farmhouse which housed the Ratchitt men. Despite it being nearly eight o'clock by the time he turned into the rutted driveway, it was still light. With daylight saving, the sun was only just setting. A dark-haired man was tinkering with a motorbike parked in the front yard. A vicious-looking black dog was barking insanely and jumping up and down on the end of a chain nearby.

As Jason drove up, Ratchitt unfolded himself from his hunched-down position, snarled at the dog to shut up, then turned to face his visitor.

Jason eyed his competition as objectively as possible. He wasn't handsome. Muriel was right about that. But he had those dark, bad-boy looks women seemed to go for in a big way. Long black hair which fell in rakish waves to his shoulders. Deep-set black eyes. And almost feminine lips. He wasn't overly tall, but his physique was all macho perfection, displayed overtly in tight stone-washed jeans and a chest-hugging black T-shirt. Jason could see without looking too hard that he was well built everywhere.

Ratchitt eyed him back as he climbed out of the car, a smug smile pulling at his full lips.

Jason wanted to wipe that smile from here to Broken Hill. But he wasn't a fool. He suddenly saw what might happen if he smashed the cocky creep's teeth in. Emma might not be impressed at all. She might tag *him* as a violent man, and run to Ratchitt's side, offering sympathy and solace.

Ratchitt's increasingly triumphant smirk told its own tale, and Jason suddenly realised he'd made a mistake in coming here. He'd fallen right into this devious fellow's hands. But it was too late now. No way was he going to back down and go off with his tail between his legs.

'The good Dr Steel, I presume?' Ratchitt drawled as Jason walked up to him.

'And the not so good Dean Ratchitt,' Jason countered drily.

Ratchitt grinned. 'The one and the same. To what do I owe the honour of this call?'

'I want you to keep away from Emma.'

'I imagine you do. But what you want and what I want are two different things, Doc.'

Jason didn't doubt it. 'She doesn't want you any more.'

He laughed. 'Is that what she told you?'

'In a word…yes.'

'Emma's always had trouble admitting what she wants.'

Jason was having trouble keeping his temper. 'I think you've lost touch with what Emma wants.'

'I don't think so, man. Her mouth *says* one thing but it *tells* you a different story. She's a good little kisser, isn't she? I taught her how. I'd have taught her a hell of a lot more if she'd let me. But that's beside the point. The point is what Emma wants.'

Jason was beginning to realise Ratchitt wasn't as dumb as he'd thought he'd be. He was a very street-smart and cunning fellow.

'You think I haven't always known what was going on in her life?' Ratchitt scoffed. 'I have eyes and ears all over Tindley. I know she never went out with anyone in all the months I was away. She was waiting for me to come back. And she'd have said yes, lick-ety-split, the next time I asked her to marry me. I was just biding my time. But then you came along, Doc, and cruelled all my plans. I made the mistake of not contacting home for a couple of months and what happened? She upped and got engaged, without so much as a single date beforehand. I'd like to know how you managed that, Doc?'

'I'll bet you would. For the record, though, I was her aunt's doctor during Ivy's last months, and a regular visitor to Emma's home. We got to know each other *very* well during that time.' And he could read into that whatever he liked!

'Oh, yes,' he sneered. 'Dear old Aunt Ivy. The stupid old bag, filling Emma with all that nonsense about no sex before marriage. She must have been out of the Dark Ages. If it hadn't been for her, Emma would have been *my* wife now, and I'd be living in clover.'

Jason frowned. In clover? What on earth was he talking about? He could not possibly think living in the back of the sweet shop would be living in clover. Or maybe he could, he rethought, glancing around at the dump he was living in.

When his gaze moved back to Ratchitt he saw that he himself was on the end of a wry appraisal.

'You know, when I first found out about you, I wondered what a fancy-pants doctor from Sydney wanted with my Emma. It couldn't be her stunning beauty, I told myself. She's a pretty little thing, but can't hold a candle to that brunette chick you used to live with.'

Jason gaped at him, and Ratchitt grinned with malicious pleasure.

'Yeah, Doc, I checked you out while you were away on your honeymoon. I checked *her* out as well. Thought it only fair. Now there's a top sort, and bloody good in the cot, even if I say so myself. Hardly had to do a thing. She told me a lot about you, too. How ambitious you were. How much money means to you. That's when it all clicked. I dare say old Aunt Ivy told you about Emma's trust fund while she was dying. It was from her parents' estate. It comes to her when she turns twenty-five, or when she gets married. Which ever happens first. Look, I don't blame you, Doc. Really I don't. But you should never poach on another man's property.'

Jason could not hide his shock. Not about Adele. He didn't give a damn about her. But about this trust fund. Emma had never mentioned it.

Any shock quickly gave way to a startling realisation.

'Good Lord! You were going to marry Emma for *money*,' he said.

Ratchitt looked taken aback by his attitude. 'Yeah, sure. Why else would anyone marry a silly little bitch like her? You didn't think I was in love with her, did you? I'm just like you, Doc. Love doesn't come into it. But I don't even have to marry her now, thanks to you. The money's there for the taking. She won't be able to deny me a thing, not once she lets me give her a bit of the old Ratchitt magic.'

Jason felt his hands begin to ball into fists.

'I hope you've done a good job in my place,' Ratchitt taunted. 'Virgins are notoriously easy to spoil, you know. They're a bit like a new bike,' he drawled, stroking the shiny black metal side as though it were a woman. 'You have to run 'em in kinda slow, or they're just never any good. Have to keep 'em well oiled too, or you're in for a bumpy ride.'

Something exploded in Jason's brain. Something white-hot and violent. Ratchitt was on the ground and out for the count before he knew what had happened. Jason was grimacing and shaking his bleeding knuckles when the cattle dog which had been chained up suddenly leapt at him, its fang-like jaws closing over his clean white shirt-sleeve, just below his elbow.

CHAPTER THIRTEEN

'Now you know what it's like to be on the other end of sutures,' Doc said as he pulled the cotton tight and reached for the scissors.

Jason had called his partner from his mobile phone, after old Jim Ratchitt had pulled the dog off him and he'd escaped into the sanctuary of his car. They'd met up at the surgery in town. No point in going to Doc's house, since it was a good fifteen-minute drive on the other side of Tindley.

Jason gritted his teeth. 'Do you have to be so rough?'

'Grown men who brawl like louts don't deserve to be treated with kid gloves.'

'A dog did this,' Jason growled. 'Not a man.'

'So you told me. You up to date with your rabies shots?'

'*What?*'

'Only joking,' Doc said, smiling through his white moustache. 'But a booster for tetanus might be a good idea. And I'll shoot you full of antibiotics for good measure.'

'How's Ratchitt, do you know?' Jason asked as Doc went about his business.

'Have no idea. What's your guess?'

'I only hit him once, but he went down like a ton of hot bricks. Must have a glass jaw.'

'Or a coward's heart. When some men go down, they stay down, till the danger's past.'

'Mmm. Do you think he might press charges?'

'No. His type don't go to the cops. They simply have you beaten up in retaliation one quiet night. Or they seduce your wife.'

Jason glowered at him. 'This town knows too damned much about everyone else's business.'

'True. But you just have to live with that. So what's the situation? Emma still hung up on that low-life?'

'Your guess is as good as mine. She says not, but the evidence isn't all in. On top of that, he's hanging around the shop and bothering her. Given his reputation with women, I find that a bit of a worry.'

'I'd be worried too. Speaking of Emma, where is she, exactly? Hard not to notice the little wife isn't here in the house, offering succour and comfort to her wounded husband.'

'She's spending a few nights at the shop. We have some things to work out.'

When Doc arched his bushy white brows, Jason gave him a narrow-eyed glare. 'And will that piece of news be on the village grapevine tomorrow?'

'Lord, Jason, you're way behind the action. That will have already done the rounds, the moment Emma's old bedroom light behind the shop went on earlier this evening.'

'I don't believe this,' he muttered.

'Then believe it. Oh, and by the way, the going odds on you and Emma divorcing are about even money. But don't worry, lad, my money's still on you. There! All done. You'll be as good as new by morning surgery.'

'Thanks a bunch.' Jason sat up and began rolling his shirt-sleeve down, till he saw it was ripped and bloodied. Muttering under his breath, he ripped the thing off and threw it in the corner, which was a pity, since it had cost a hundred bucks.

'Tch-tch,' Doc said as he tidied up the consultation table. 'Emma won't like that. She's a meticulous girl, is Emma.'

'Well, too bad! She isn't here to notice anyway, is she? I can be a slob if I want to be.'

'You can be an idiot if you want to be too. Why don't you go down there and tell her you love her?'

Jason's eyes whipped round to stare at him.

Doc shrugged. 'We all know your marriage wasn't a love match in the beginning. But I'm betting you love her now. She's a treasure, is our Emma. Only selfish, ignorant bums like Dean Ratchitt can't appreciate that.'

Jason considered the suggestion for what it was worth, then discarded it. 'She won't believe me.'

'Why not?'

'Partly because she thinks I still love another woman.'

'Just like you think *she* loves Ratchitt. Looks like we have two fools here instead of one.'

Jason frowned. Could Doc be right? Could Emma have fallen in love with *him*?

'Don't let too much water run under the bridge before you tell her, Jason. Dean won't be. You mark my words. I didn't like to mention this before, but I heard a motorbike rumble down the street a little while back. You were in too much pain to notice. If you don't want to lose Emma for good, then I suggest you hotfoot it down to the shop before this evening's incident is given a slant you won't recognise.'

Jason felt sick at the thought, but confused at the same time. 'How would he know she was there and not here...with me? She only left at tea-time.'

'I dare say he got the news from Sheryl.

'Sheryl lives on the other side of the sweet shop,' Doc elaborated when Jason looked even more confused. 'She's a legal secretary, works for Jack Winters, Ivy's solicitor. Went out with Dean, briefly a couple of years back. She's a good bit older than Dean but not bad looking. And she's never married. Probably still fancies him.'

Jason thought of Dean's boast that he had eyes and ears all over Tindley. Who better to tell him about Emma than a next-door neighbour?

'I have to go and get a fresh shirt first,' he said, heading for the door.

'Don't go getting into another fight!'

'I'll do what I have to do to protect Emma from that creep.'

Doc sighed. 'You do realise I'm getting too old for all this drama.'

'Then retire, and I'll get myself a new partner,' Jason tossed over his shoulder as he hurried from the room.

'You and what army?' Doc called after him.

Jason grabbed the first shirt he could find. It just happened to be a black designer number which had probably cost more than Ratchitt's whole bloody wardrobe. He was still tucking it into the waistband of his grey trousers as he bolted down the stairs and ran from the house.

He didn't knock on Emma's back door. He bowled straight in, sucking in a sharp breath when he saw a decidedly worse-for-wear Ratchitt sitting at the kitchen table. The right hand side of his chin was swollen, and there was an ugly bruise spoiling his macho perfection. He'd never seen a better target for a woman's pity, whereas *his* wounds were well hidden.

Emma was at the kitchen sink when Jason burst in. She whirled, worry filling her face as her eyes searched *his*.

'See?' Ratchitt taunted straight away. 'Not a mark on him. He jumped me when I wasn't looking, Emma. The man's mad. And violent. He tried to kill me. If it wasn't for my dog, he might have.'

'The world wouldn't be any the less for your death, Ratchitt,' Jason grated out. 'But it won't be me who does the deed. You're not worth spending twenty years in jail for. Emma, don't believe a word he tells you. The man's totally without conscience. He told me this evening that his only interest in you was money, some trust fund you came into when you married. He called you a silly little bitch and said he'd never loved you. He also bragged that now he wouldn't have to marry you to get the money. He thinks he can seduce you, then con you out of it.'

She didn't say a word, just stared at him with startled, disbelieving eyes.

'Just about word for word, wasn't it, honey?'
Ratchitt drawled, rising to his feet and going over to
a frozen Emma, placing a triumphantly possessive
arm around her shoulders and drawing her to his side.
'But it wasn't me saying any of that filth, you bastard,' he sneered at Jason. 'It was you, as you very
well know.'

Ratchitt tipped Emma's face up to his with a gentle
little gesture. 'He boasted to me that he'd twist it all
around and make out I said I wanted to marry you for
the money,' he told her, stunning Jason with the passionate sincerity in his voice and eyes. 'But honest,
Emma, I didn't know anything about this trust fund.
You think your aunt would have told *me* about such
a thing? She might have told *him*, though,' he went
on, pointing an accusing finger at Jason. 'He probably
got her to confide in him when she was in a morphine
daze. And what did he do? As soon as she was dead,
he proposed. That proposal was a shock, wasn't it?
He hadn't given you any indication that he cared for
you before, had he?'

Jason watched, appalled, as Emma slowly shook
her head.

'I thought not. He lied to me about that, too. When
I tackled him on the suddenness of your engagement,
he said it wasn't at all sudden, that you'd become
great friends during his visits to your aunt. More than
friends, actually. He implied you'd become lovers.'

Her eyes flew to Jason's, pained and reproachful.
Groaning, he did his best to adopt an aggrieved expression, but he had a feeling he just looked furious.

'I didn't tell you this earlier, Emma,' Ratchitt was

saying, 'but after you went away on your honeymoon I went to Sydney to check up on this man you married. I was worried about you. What did you know of him, really? I found this colleague of his, who turned out to be his old girlfriend, and what she told me about him made my hair curl. The man's a cold-blooded, mercenary monster. Money is his god, Emma. He'd do anything for it. Say anything. Marry anyone. On top of that he's violent, as you can see. I still love you, Emma, despite everything. But he doesn't. He'll hurt you, Emma. Let me move in here to protect you from him. Let me look after you and love you as you deserve to be loved.'

'No!' Jason cried.

'It's not up to you, Steel,' Ratchitt snapped.

Jason looked straight at Emma with an imploring gaze. 'Please, Emma, I beg of you. You don't have to come back to me yet, if you don't want to, but don't let him into your life, not for a moment.'

'How...how did you know about the trust fund?' she choked out.

Jason grimaced. 'I didn't. Not till Ratchitt told me tonight.'

'Yeah, right,' Dean sneered. 'As if I'd do that if I *did* know.'

'You knew all right,' Jason said with sudden inspiration. 'Your friend Sheryl told you. She works for your aunt's solicitor, Emma, and lives next door. Doc told me she and Dean were lovers once. She's still crazy about him and would tell him anything he wanted to know. She must have told him you were here, and not up at my house. Why else did he come *here* tonight, instead of the surgery? Someone had to tell him. I certainly didn't. Did you?'

'N…no.'

'Then ask him. Ask him why he came here.'

'Dean?'

'He's grabbing at straws, Emma. Sheryl didn't tell me anything of the kind. *He* did. That's why he came looking for me out at the farm. Because you'd left him and he was worried stiff you'd find out he never loved you.'

'Jason never promised to love me,' she said in a puzzled voice.

'And neither will he,' Ratchitt insisted. 'Ever!'

'That's not true,' Jason denied with an anguished groan. 'Not true,' he repeated, his shoulders sagging as his heart began to despair. 'I *do* love you, Emma. I love you with all my heart. I didn't marry you for any money. I knew nothing of any trust fund till I heard about it from Ratchitt tonight. He thinks all men are tarred with the same brush. He couldn't seem to imagine my actually loving you. Yet I cannot imagine *not* loving you. I certainly can't imagine my life without you.'

Jason knew he wasn't being very impressive with his declaration of love. His voice sounded tired and defeated, probably because of the look on her face. The shock and the patent disbelief. He was wasting his breath. Totally wasting his breath.

'I can't make you love me back,' he continued, driven on by desperation, not any real hope. 'I can't make you come home with me. I can't make you stay away from this…creature. All I can do is appeal to your common sense. I know you have heaps. Think, Emma. Think and judge. A man is known by his actions, not his words. Would I have acted as I have acted this past few weeks if I hadn't been sick with a very real jealousy? And would Ratchitt have acted as he has acted this past year if he really loved you?'

She didn't say a word, just kept staring at him.

He sighed. 'That's all I have to say. That's all there *is* to say. I'm going home now. I'll wait for you till morning. If you don't come, I won't be staying in Tindley. I couldn't bear it. You can have a divorce. You can have *him*, if he's what you really want. I won't stand in your way. But God have pity on your soul if that's the way you choose, Emma, because he'll destroy you.'

'Don't listen to him, Emma. He's the one who'll destroy you. He's evil. And clever. Far cleverer than me. I don't have his power with words. Or his fancy education. I only have what's in my heart. Feel this heart, Emma,' Dean Ratchitt said, taking her hand and placing it on his chest. 'It's beating for you. I know I hurt you a year ago. I was wrong. All I can say is that I was lonely for you, and that girl threw herself at me. But that wasn't love, Emma. That was just sex. Surely you can see what I mean now. You've been to bed with this man. You've had sex with him. But that's not making love. That doesn't come from the heart. When we're finally together, *that* will be making love. It'll be incredible, princess. I promise you...'

She was staring up into those penetrating black eyes of his as though hypnotised, seemingly unable to break away from the sexual spell his words and his presence were casting over her body. Jason could not bear to watch it any more. His heart was breaking.

He turned and walked through the back door, stumbling a little on the steps. Somehow, he made it back up the street and into the surgery.

Doc had left, thank God. He would not have wanted another man to see the tears streaming down his face. He made it into the living room, where he slumped into the big armchair to the right of the empty hearth. He didn't turn on the reading lamp next to it, just sat there in the semi-darkness staring into nothingness, the tears slowly drying on his face as the minutes ticked away. For a while his ear strained to catch the sound of Emma's steps on the front porch, his heart aching with one last, final, futile hope.

How could she not see the truth? How could she be taken in by that creep?

Easily, Jason finally accepted. As easily as he had been taken in by Adele all those years. Both of them had outer physical attractions which could mask the ugly person inside. Both were clever and cunning. Both dared to do what decent people would not even dream of doing. They conned and corrupted. They seduced and schemed.

Jason's thoughts finally turned to Emma, and he knew he shouldn't sit by and let Ratchitt taint such a beautiful person. But what could he do, short of killing the bloke?

Nothing, really. In days gone by he could have kidnapped her and carried her off to some faraway land, but not nowadays. Nowadays, that would land him in jail. But wouldn't jail be preferable to this agony of doing nothing to save her from a fate worse than death?

He was still sitting there, mentally tossing up between murder and kidnapping, when he heard the sound of the front door opening.

CHAPTER FOURTEEN

JASON's hands balled into fists on the armrests of the chair. He dared not get his hopes up. What if he was wrong? What if she'd just come home to get some clothes? What if it wasn't Emma at all?

He sat there like a block of stone, petrified.

'Jason?' Emma called softly. 'Where are you?'

He didn't answer. Couldn't.

He listened to her walk up the stairs and call out to him there listened as she walked slowly back down. 'Jason, where *are* you?' she cried again at the bottom of the stairs, sounding almost despairing.

'I'm in here,' he said at last, but his voice sounded odd. Empty and hollow.

She switched on the light, then just stood there in the doorway, looking over at him. He didn't know what he looked like, but it must have been pretty terrible by the expression on her face.

'Oh, Jason,' she groaned, and ran over to squat down by the chair.

'I'm sorry,' she cried, her green eyes filling while his remained strangely dry and distant. 'So very sorry...'

Jason's chest was aching. She was sorry. Sorry about what? Sorry she was leaving him?

That had to be it. She'd taken too long to come home for the outcome to be otherwise. It was agony

166

thinking of what she and Ratchitt had been doing during that time.

'Just get whatever it is you've come for,' he said flatly. 'And go.' He no longer had any stomach for his earlier violent solutions. If she was fool enough to want Ratchitt, then let her be destroyed. Why not? He was.

'But I've come home, Jason,' she said. 'I chose you.' And, reaching out, she touched him on the arm, right where the dog had bitten him.

He wrenched his arm away, his moan a mixture of emotional and physical pain.

'What is it?' she said, her eyes instantly stricken. 'What's wrong with your arm? Show me!' Already she was undoing his cuff and gently peeling back the sleeve. Her gasp was horrified. Jason looked down at it closely for the first time himself.

It *did* look pretty nasty, despite Doc's expert handiwork. Much worse than Ratchitt's face. He would carry scars for the rest of his life.

'Oh, Jason...'

'It'll be all right,' he said sharply.

Their eyes met, but he still could not quite believe what she'd said. 'You meant it?' he rasped. 'About coming home? About choosing me?'

She nodded, and two big tears trickled down her face.

'What about Ratchitt?'

'I sent him away.'

'You sent him away,' he repeated dazedly.

'I don't love him any more, Jason. I don't even want him any more.'

'You don't?'

'No. I'm sure of that, Jason. Quite sure.'

He couldn't say anything to that, his heart too awash with emotion.

'You…didn't just say that about loving me, did you?' she asked. 'You did mean it, didn't you?'

'Yes.' That was all he could manage. Just yes. His relief was too intense, his exhaustion total.

She nodded. 'I didn't think you would lie about something like that. Not you.' And, taking the hand of his good arm, she began tugging him to his feet.

'What are you doing?' he choked out.

'I'm taking my husband upstairs to bed. He looks tired.'

'Tired' did not begin to describe the state he was in.

He let her lead him upstairs, let her sit him down on the side of the bed while she knelt down at his feet and began taking off his shoes and socks.

He wanted to ask her what had happened with Ratchitt after he left. He wanted to ask her about the trust fund. But he didn't have the energy. Or the will. Instead, he watched her tend to him with a sweet gentleness which threatened to embarrass him for ever in front of her. Only with the greatest force of will did he keep his own tears at bay.

At last he was naked, and being tipped back under cool sheets. 'Can I get you anything?' she asked. 'A glass of water? Some painkillers?'

'Painkillers would be good. There are some extra strong ones lying on my desk in the surgery. Just bring me the packet.'

He closed his eyes after she left the room and began counting to ten. If he got to ten without crying, he thought, everything would be all right.

He didn't cry. But he didn't get to ten, either. Something very strange happened to him around eight. He fell asleep.

Jason woke to the feel of Emma's arm sliding around his waist, plus the tips of her breasts pressing into his back. For a moment, everything inside him leapt, till her deep even breathing told him she was actually asleep. Understandable, he accepted, after a quick glance at the bedside clock.

It was five past two.

For a long while, he lay there in the dark, mulling over everything that had happened the night before, still stunned by the outcome. Emma had chosen *him*, not Ratchitt. She didn't love Ratchitt any more.

It was almost too good to be true. What had changed her mind about Ratchitt? What had happened after he'd left them alone together?

Her apology when she'd first come home took on a sinister meaning. What had she been saying sorry for? Had she let Ratchitt make love to her, only to find out her fantasies about him had been just that— fantasies?

Something must have happened during the time which had elapsed. He couldn't see Ratchitt wasting time just talking to Emma. That was not his style.

But being unfaithful wasn't Emma's style, either. He knew that, down deep in his heart. No, something else had happened to make her see the light.

And the light was what? *He* was a better bet for

the future than Ratchitt? Jason dared not hope she'd suddenly discovered she loved him. That was the hope of fools. More likely she'd chosen the lesser of two evils.

He still felt terrible about the way he'd acted since they'd arrived home in Tindley. He could not blame her for leaving him. He'd treated her without consideration and without respect. Without love.

Emma stirred against his back, snuggling in closer, murmuring his name in her sleep. When she lifted her leg to hook it over his, Jason was taken aback to discover she was totally naked. She hadn't come to bed like that since their honeymoon, he recalled.

Back then, he'd rolled over many times during the night to make love to her. And it had been so wonderful. At least in bed he could make her happy.

He went to roll over right then and there...till the pain in his arm momentarily stopped him.

But only momentarily. It seemed an aching arm was no deterrent to the waves of desire which began flooding through him. Jason suspected his arm could be falling off and nothing would stop him wanting to make love to her.

Slowly, carefully, he rolled over. Instinctively, she rolled too. Yet she was still asleep. Jason curved himself around her, keeping his damaged arm out of harm's way. He slid his other arm under her, tipping her slightly backwards against his chest, bringing her breasts within easy reach.

She woke slowly, voluptuously, arching her back into his hands, showing him with her body language that she liked what he was doing. More than liked it.

Her arms lifted above her head to find and wind around his neck, leaving both her breasts, and the entire front of her body, unhindered for his pleasure. Her right knee lifted up onto his right thigh, opening and offering herself for whatever he might want.

Her attitude of total sexual surrender sent his desire for her off the Richter scale. Not to mention his love. Even if she didn't love him back, she'd chosen him. And she wanted him, wanted him more than a man she'd claimed she would always love and *never* forget. Surely that must mean it was only a matter of time before she was his, totally. His heart swelled with passionate determination. He would make love to her with every ounce of skill he had, showing her that, despite his own runaway passion, *her* pleasure would be his first priority from now on. He wanted to wipe away the memory of the past couple of weeks when he'd been so abominable to her.

Carefully, he eased himself inside her, his hands splaying across her stomach to keep her still against him. But her insides weren't still, and for a panic-stricken moment he feared disaster. Hell, he was drowning in her heat, being seduced by her pulsating muscles. The pleasure was dizzying, and potentially destructive.

No way could he last.

But he was going to, no matter what!

'Emma, be still,' he warned her sharply, when she began squeezing and releasing him between frantic little wriggles of her bottom.

'I can't,' she gasped, and came with an intensity which threatened his resolve to give her the experience of a lifetime. It took every ounce of his will not to let everything come to a swift and premature end right then and there.

Gradually, her spasms died away, and he set to making love to her seriously, with a steady rhythm, using his hands to re-arouse her. Her second climax was gentler on him, but no less difficult to ignore. He ploughed on, taking her on to the highest of pleasure zones, where her whole body was so sensitised that the slightest touch of his knowing fingertip had her quivering with delight. Only when he knew he could not last another moment did he take her with him to a third full-blown orgasm.

'Oh, Jason,' she cried afterwards as he cradled her to him, her body still trembling. 'Jason...'

'Hush, my darling,' he murmured as he rocked her gently to and fro. 'Relax... Go to sleep...'

'I can't. I... I...'

'Shh. Don't talk. Just take deep breaths, then let go all your muscles.'

She did as he suggested, scooping in then letting out several huge, shuddering sighs. Her arms and legs finally went very limp.

'Sleepy,' she mumbled.

'Yes,' he agreed, stroking her hair.

Once she was unconscious, Jason eased himself from her. Rolling over, he reached for the painkillers she'd left on the bedside chest and which he hadn't taken earlier. He took three. Hell, he needed them. His arm felt as if a mad dog had mauled it, and the rest of him wasn't much better.

But he was content. More content than he'd ever

been in all his life. She might not love him yet, but she would…in time. Ratchitt was history.

Carefully, he rolled back over onto his side and curved his aching arm around the sleeping form beside him.

She didn't stir an inch. Thank God.

CHAPTER FIFTEEN

JASON woke to the dawn…and more pain. His arm felt as if it had been put through a shredder. His head was aching, as was his whole body.

A sidewards glance showed a curled up Emma, sleeping like a baby.

'It's all your fault,' he muttered under his breath, but with a wry smile forming. 'You've totally wrecked me.'

The wreck struggled out from under the covers and staggered downstairs to the surgery, where he dressed the wound, gave himself another shot of antibiotics and swallowed some bigger pain-killing bombs. Only his nudity prevented Jason from wandering out onto the front porch and watching the sun rise. He didn't want to scandalise the people of Tindley any more than he'd already scandalised them. No doubt the news of the night before would be doing the rounds of the town with a speed and inaccuracy which would rival Peyton Place.

Oh, well. At least everything had come out all right. In a fashion. Emma was back home in his bed and Ratchitt was…gone, he hoped. Permanently.

Jason levered himself back upstairs, where he literally ran into Emma, hurrying through their bedroom door in her birthday suit.

'Oh, there you are, Jason!' she exclaimed. 'I woke

up and you were gone. I was worried. What have you been doing downstairs? Did you want something? A cup of tea, perhaps? Some breakfast?'

She was babbling, he could see. And blushing. God, he liked it when she blushed.

'Let's go back to bed,' he said, taking her arm and praying those painkillers kicked in shortly.

Her upward gaze betrayed she was not averse to his suggestion. 'But…but what about your poor arm?' she protested feebly.

His smile was wry. 'You weren't too worried about my poor arm in the middle of the night.'

She blushed some more, but her eyes carried warm memories of their lovemaking. 'That was…incredible, Jason. But then, I knew it would be.'

His eyebrows lifted. 'You did? How come?'

'Oh, Jason…' She placed her hands, palms down, upon his chest, reaching up to kiss him lightly on the mouth. 'You were the one who said sex could be extremely satisfying without love, remember?'

His insides tightened. 'Yes,' he said tautly. 'I remember.'

'But you added that being in love would enhance the experience.'

He stared down at her, that horrible thing called hope doing awful things to his stomach. 'What are you trying to say, Emma?'

'I love you, Jason.'

He swallowed a couple of times. 'You…you wouldn't say a thing like that unless you meant it, would you?'

'Never in a million years, my darling.'

Oh, God…

Only her lips saved him, her lovely, loving lips, kissing away the shock, taking him back from the threshold of total embarrassment to that place reserved for lovers where their bodies and hearts beat as one and nothing existed but their love and need for each other. They moved together onto the bed to show that love and satisfy their need as man and woman had since the garden of Eden. Afterwards, they lay locked in each other's arms, basking in the afterglow of their lovemaking.

Jason felt no pain, only the sweetest of pleasures and the deepest of wonders. Emma loved him. Everything *was* going to be all right.

'When did you know you loved me?' he asked her, wonder still in his voice.

'I suspected as much after that incident with Adele,' came her astonishing reply, 'but I wasn't certain till last night.'

'When last night?'

'I'm not sure when, exactly. Last night carried a lot of confusion. Your declaration of love stunned me, Jason. I could not quite believe it. To be honest, I've had trouble believing in our relationship from the word go. It all seemed rather…unreal.'

'Unreal, Emma? In what way?'

'Do you have no idea, Jason, how you present yourself to others? Or how you might look to a simple country girl? That first day you came to visit Aunt Ivy, I took one look at you and I thought…wow!'

Jason was staggered. 'But you didn't even *look* at me!'

'Oh, yes, I did. Sneakily. And I thought about you afterwards. But not in any real way. You were like some movie star. Way out of my league, but nice to dream about. I found myself looking forward to your visits, just so I could look at you some more. I used to wonder what you were doing here in our little country town, with your trendy clothes, your city sophistication and your incredible style. I tried to picture what kind of woman you'd end of marrying if you stayed. That was why I was so shocked when you asked me. I didn't fit the image I'd made up for your wife in my mind...

'But Adele did,' she went on. 'She fitted it like a glove. God, that weekend was ghastly. I don't know how I survived it. I'd been wanting you to make love to me so badly, and I was missing you terribly, when suddenly there was this gorgeous woman standing in my dreary little shop, telling me you would never be faithful to boring little me and that she'd spent most of the weekend in bed with you. When she left I wanted to smash everything in sight. I was so eaten up with jealousy, I couldn't see straight. Nothing else she'd said seemed to matter, only that you'd made love to *her*, and not me. In the end, I just cried and cried and cried. That was when I knew I was far more emotionally involved with you than I'd realised.'

Jason could empathise with everything she felt— and he did. 'I was the same, believe me,' he said feelingly. 'The panic I felt when I found out Adele had been to see you was incredible. I should have known I loved you back then. Instead, it didn't hit me till I saw you walking down the aisle on our wedding day. I was quite blown away, I can tell you.'

Emma shook her head. 'I probably would have felt the same way about you that day, if I hadn't been worried sick about Dean causing trouble. It wasn't till we were well away from Tindley that I could relax and begin to enjoy being married to you. And I did enjoy it, Jason. Even when I didn't know I loved you.'

'The sex, you mean?'

'Yes. Was that wicked of me?'

'Not at all. Just human. You were ripe and ready to be made love to, Emma. I thank my lucky stars that I came along at the right time in your life.'

'I'm glad I waited for you, Jason. I'm glad to never made love with Dean. I love you much more than I ever loved him.'

His heart tripped over. 'You make me ashamed of myself for the way I've treated you these past couple of weeks. My only excuse—and it sounds pathetic— is that I was crazy with insecurity and jealousy.'

'You need never be jealous of Dean again, Jason. I despise him. I'm well aware that everything he ever told me was a lie, including what he said about you last night. Not that I didn't already suspect as much.'

'But I thought you were totally taken in by him! The way you were looking up at him, like you were hypnotised.'

'Not hypnotised, Jason. Shocked. Too much had happened too quickly. I felt totally disorientated. It was only when you walked out that my mind began to clear. I still wasn't convinced of your love for me. I was worried you might just be trying to get me back with words. But I began to see that everything you'd said about Dean did make sense. His past actions certainly weren't those of a man genuinely in love. His attitude once you'd left didn't endear him to me, either. He became insufferably smug and presumptuous. When he started manhandling me, and telling her how much he loved me, I found myself rejecting his declaration of love much more strongly than I had yours.'

Jason frowned. 'What do you mean...manhandling you?'

'Oh, you know. Hugging me and kissing me.'

'You let him *kiss* you?'

'I didn't *let* him do anything. He just did it.'

'I'll kill him!'

'No, you won't. I don't want you going to jail over that trash. Look, I'm glad I let him kiss me one last time, Jason, because I didn't like it one bit. In fact, I found it quite repulsive. I knew then I felt nothing for him any more, not even a sexual attraction. When he kept insisting that my inheritance meant nothing to him, I just knew he was lying. I wanted him out of my life, and out of Tindley. For ever. But I knew he was not about to give up, not while he thought I was rich. There was no use just saying go away, that I didn't love him any more. Frankly, Jason, I'd already said as much to him on our wedding day, and he simply took no notice. So I told him I was relieved he wasn't interested in my money, because the trustees of my fund had invested all my money into the Asian money market and they'd lost the lot in the 1997 crash.'

'And had they?'

'No, of course not. But that's beside the point. Once I said that, you should have seen him back-pedal as fast as he could. Suddenly, my irresistible charms became very resistible. He started talking about how it might not be a good idea if he moved in with me just yet because it might ruin my reputation, and he cared about me too much to do that. He said it might be better if we waited till I got a divorce. When I calmly told him I had no intention of getting a divorce, and that I'd decided to go back to you, he blustered a bit about women never knowing their own minds, and that he would never have come back to Tindley except for me. I then told him that perhaps it might be better if he left Tindley, after which he pretended to be angry and stormed out of the house. He was riding off down the road without a backward glance as I walked up here to you. I doubt he'll be back. He's exhausted Tindley's supply of eligible females. I think he'll try greener pastures.'

Jason didn't doubt it. With a bit of luck, he'd go back to Sydney and look up Adele again. They deserved each other.

He thought of telling Emma about Ratchitt and Adele, but decided there was no point any more. Besides, the last thing he wanted was to keep bringing up old history. Let sleeping dogs lie...

'Three million,' Emma said abruptly, interrupting his thoughts.

'Three million what?'

'Three million dollars. That's how much my trust fund is worth, give or take a few thousand.'

Jason saw the worry in her face and understood it.

'I knew nothing about this trust fund, Jason,' she elaborated, 'till after Aunt Ivy's death. She left me a letter in her will about it. She also advised me strongly never to tell anyone about the money. Not till after I was safely married, anyway.'

Jason could appreciate Aunt Ivy's common sense. But Emma's eyes still bothered him. 'She never told me about it, Emma,' he insisted. 'Honest.'

'Oh, I know that. I'm just worried the money might change things between us.'

'I see...' And he surely did. Money corrupted. 'Give it away, Emma,' he said firmly. 'Donate it to some charity. Cancer research, perhaps.'

Her sigh carried a telling amount of relief. 'I'm so glad you said that. I was thinking the very same thing. Of course, I might keep a little nest-egg, just for emergencies. But the bulk of it can go.'

'Splendid idea!'

'Oh, Jason!' she cried, hugging him tightly. 'I do so love you. I felt so terrible when I came home last night and saw you sitting in that armchair, looking so devastated. I think that was the first moment I really believed you loved me.'

'And you, Emma? Did you know then that you loved me back?'

'I'm sure I did, but I just couldn't seem to face it. I don't know why. Perhaps I was afraid to. Then, later, when you made love to me like you did, I...I was just...overwhelmed. But I knew how much I loved you the moment I woke and found you gone. Oh, I knew it then, Jason.'

He could understand that. There was something

about loss—even a temporary one—which stripped the wool from one's eyes.

'I love you with all my heart,' she said sincerely.

His own heart filled to overflowing. 'Tell me again.'

'I love you.'

'And I love you, dear, sweet Emma. I love everything about you, even your stubbornness.'

Her eyes flickered with surprise. 'My stubbornness? I'm not stubborn.'

'Oh, yes, you are, my darling. But that's all right. I wouldn't want you too perfect.'

'I'm far from perfect.'

'Not too far,' he murmured, and his mother's words echoed in his mind once more.

You can't have everything in life, son.

But he knew that you could, if what you wanted were the simple things in life. And if you were lucky enough to marry a girl like Emma.

'Jason…'

'Yes?'

'I…um…didn't go on the pill.'

'That's good.'

'You know, it worries me a bit, not getting pregnant after all the sex we had. Do you think something could be wrong with me?'

Jason felt his heart catch. But he kept quite calm. Worry and tension were not advisable when a couple were trying for a baby. 'Now why should there be something wrong with you?' he said reassuringly. 'Or me, for that matter? These things take time, love.' And he gave her a comforting squeeze.

'Oh!' she gasped, and smiled a wide smile up at him. 'That's it, Jason!'

'What's it?'

'Love! Before, we were just having sex. But now...now we're making love. We'll make a baby this month. I'm sure of it.'

He forced himself to smile. 'I'll certainly give it my best shot.'

It was the most difficult month of Jason's life. Keeping his emotional cool while making love to Emma till he was exhausted. As the day approached when her period was due, he was beside himself with tension. Which was crazy. Because what he'd said to her was true. These things *did* sometimes take time. Lots of it. To put this kind of pressure on himself at this stage was silly, and potentially destructive.

D-day arrived and went. No period. Another day. Then another. And another. Jason knew he could do a pregnancy test on her—they were accurate far earlier these days—but he didn't dare suggest it. That would betray his escalating tension. And make a big issue of her conceiving.

He was getting ready for afternoon surgery the next day when Emma suddenly burst in, waving something in her hands. 'It was positive, Jason!' she cried excitedly. 'We're pregnant! I bought a test from the chemist. The one being advertised in all the women's magazines. It said you could tell at ten days, and I'm well over that.'

Joy and relief exploded through his chest like a

fireworks display. He hadn't realised till that moment how much having a family of his own meant to him.

Unable to express his feelings in words, he scooped her up into his arms and kissed her over and over.

'Just as well Nancy's stepped outside to do some shopping,' he said breathlessly, when he finally put her down again. 'Otherwise the whole of Tindley would know the news before this day was out.'

Emma gave him a pitying look, then laughed.

'What are you laughing at?'

'Jason, everyone already knows.'

'But how? Did you tell them?'

'No. But they're past masters at putting two and two together. Not that it would have been hard. There's only one chemist shop in Tindley. What would you think if a recently married person—namely me—came in and bought a pregnancy testing kit, then half an hour later went running from her shop up the street like a madwoman into her doctor husband's surgery?'

Jason pulled a face. 'She's pregnant?'

'Exactly!'

He sighed. 'Maybe you shouldn't bother to have an ultrasound at four months. We'll just ask the good ladies of Tindley. No doubt they'll operate a book, giving odds on the sex, the due date, weight length and name! Did you know we were even money on getting a divorce at one stage?' Jason began shaking his head. 'That's the only drawback to living in Tindley. That infernal grapevine!'

'True,' Emma said, nodding sagely. 'But it's much

better than living in the city. You can't have everything in life, Jason. Everyone knows that.'

He blinked at her, then laughed.

'What did I say that was so funny?'

'Nothing.'

She gave him a suspicious look. 'You're not keeping secrets from me again, are you?'

'Never! It's just that that was what my mother always used to say. That you can't have everything in
life.'

'And it's true.'

Jason looked at this beautiful girl who loved him
and who was carrying his child and drew her into his
arms once more.

'No, it's not, my darling. Not in my case. Because
I have you, and you are everything.'

She looked up at him with wonder in her eyes. 'Do
you want our baby to be a boy or a girl?'

'I don't mind either way. Do you?'

'No. Any child of yours will be special. Thank you
for marrying me, Jason. Thank you for saving me
from myself.'

Jason knew who should be thanking whom, but he
was a man, after all, and allowed his ego to wallow
in her lovely words. 'You're welcome, my darling,'
he murmured, and slowly, gently, covered her mouth
with his.

It was a girl. Emma named her Juliette, in keeping
with the Steel tradition of using names starting with
J. Only one person in Tindley collected on the name.
A charge of 'insider information' was directed at

Nancy, but she claimed innocence. She'd simply chosen the most romantic name she could think of!

Juliette's christening was an all-town affair, with Jason's brother, Jerry, and the Brandewildes the proud godparents. Jerry had come to Tindley at Emma's instigation, late in her pregnancy, when she'd said she needed help in the shop. Jerry had proved to be a born sweet-seller, his shyness eventually evaporating with life in a smaller and much friendlier community. Emma had given him the rooms behind the shop to live in, shifting her plans for a craft club to the local hall.

At Juliette's christening, her proud dad brought forth his new video camera, bought for him by his doting wife from that little nest-egg she'd put aside. Emma was always buying Jason things. A lovely sapphire dress ring. The latest VC player. A super-soft leather reading chair with footrest. He loved being spoiled by her, and loved spoiling her back again in his own special way!

The people of Tindley counted their blessings every time they saw the happy family walking down the main street together. Dr Steel was going to stay, the men of Tindley finally agreed. No doubt about that.

The matter was deemed as settled, and money changed hands. The odds on Jason staying had been a generous four to one when the bets were first laid eighteen months before.

Doc Brandewilde really cleaned up.

HARLEQUIN® *Presents*

The world's bestselling romance series... The series that brings you your favorite authors, month after month:

Helen Bianchin
Emma Darcy
Lynne Graham
Penny Jordan
Miranda Lee
Sandra Marton
Anne Mather
Carole Mortimer
Susan Napier
Michelle Reid

and many more uniquely talented authors!

Wealthy, powerful, gorgeous men...Women who have feelings just like your own... The stories you love, set in glamorous, international locations

HARLEQUIN PRESENTS®
Seduction and passion guaranteed!

Available wherever Harlequin books are sold.

Princes...Princesses...
London Castles...New York Mansions...
To live the life of a royal!

In 2002, Harlequin Books lets you escape to a world of royalty with these royally themed titles:

Temptation:
January 2002—*A Prince of a Guy* (#861)
February 2002—*A Noble Pursuit* (#865)

American Romance:
The Carradignes: American Royalty (Editorially linked series)
March 2002—*The Improperly Pregnant Princess* (#913)
April 2002—*The Unlawfully Wedded Princess* (#917)
May 2002—*The Simply Scandalous Princess* (#921)
November 2002—*The Inconveniently Engaged Prince* (#945)

Intrigue:
The Carradignes: A Royal Mystery (Editorially linked series)
June 2002—*The Duke's Covert Mission* (#666)

Chicago Confidential
September 2002—*Prince Under Cover* (#678)

The Crown Affair
October 2002—*Royal Target* (#682)
November 2002—*Royal Ransom* (#686)
December 2002—*Royal Pursuit* (#690)

Harlequin Romance:
June 2002—*His Majesty's Marriage* (#3703)
July 2002—*The Prince's Proposal* (#3709)

Harlequin Presents:
August 2002—*Society Weddings* (#2268)
September 2002—*The Prince's Pleasure* (#2274)

Duets:
September 2002—*Once Upon a Tiara/Henry Ever After* (#83)
October 2002—*Natalia's Story/Andrea's Story* (#85)

 Celebrate a year of royalty with Harlequin Books!

Available at your favorite retail outlet.

HARLEQUIN®
Makes any time special ®

Visit us at www.eHarlequin.com

HSROY02